When it's all RELATIVE

Therese Szymanski

Bella
BOOKS

2008

Bella Books, Inc.
P.O. Box 10543
Tallahassee, FL 32302

Printed in the United States of America on acid-free paper
First Edition

Editor: Cindy Cresap
Cover designer: Stephanie Solomon-Lopez

ISBN-10: 1-59493-109-7
ISBN-13: 978-1-59493-109-3

For Mark Szymanski
10/3/1950–9/2/2007
My eldest brother, who was also my godfather, obviously had nothing
in common with any of Brett's brothers.
I loved him, and I miss him. And I hope he approves of the sword we
sent him on to the next world with.

Acknowledgments

As always, of course, I adore Linda Hill and all of Bella's staff, including Sara and Becky and all the folks who make the magic happen.

Cindy Cresap is a wonderful editor who is willing to call me on all my crap and step aside when she's sure I might get pounded by folks for some ridiculous thing that's entirely my own fault. It's absolutely brilliant to have someone like her who will thwap me when I need it and catches so much of my crap.

Speaking of . . . Thanks also to Ruth Stanley and Deana Casamento, the fantabulous Bella proofers who helped me on this. Good proofers really help me to not look quite as foolish as I do in real life, and I'm most appreciative of such!

Also, I'd like to thank my fellow Bella author, Terri Breneman, for rushing in to help me when things got rough. A case of beer brought in a cooler when I'm at a conference in another town while under severe deadline pressure can definitely help me get the book done.

And last, but obviously not least, my wonderful girlfriend, Stacia. She really does call me on my shit, and will thwap me about any linguistic crap I pull that doesn't work. She also supports me when I'm doing my "Oh my God, what have I gotten myself into?" dance. I love you, baby!

About the Author

Therese (Reese) Szymanski is a writer. During the day she writes and edits for a national nonprofit organization, and at night she writes her own stuff. She's an award-winning playwright and has been short-listed for a couple of Lammys, Goldies and a Spectrum, and made the Publishing Triangle's list of Notable Lesbian Books with her first anthology. She is the recipient of a 2008 Alice B. Readers' Appreciation award, and is an active member of Mystery Writers of America (MWA) and a member of Romance Writers of America (RWA).

She's edited a bunch of books, worked on some team books, written a bunch of books on her own, and had a few dozen shorter works published in a wide variety of books (mostly erotica, but some essays and other pieces as well). She's also written reviews, humor columns, feature pieces, interview stories and a bunch of other things for a lot of different publications.

You can e-mail Reese at tsszymanski@worldnet.att.net, and she keeps a very silly LiveJournal about totally nonsensical things at http://reeseszymanski.livejournal.com. Her new Web site is at www.BigBadButch.com.

When she's not writing, editing, designing, playing with her sword collection or committing other acts of mayhem, she spends time with her girlfriend, Stacia.

Prologue
1993

Brett was sitting at her desk, writing up the dancers' schedule for the next month and talking with her girlfriend, Allie, on the phone when a shriek broke through the unfaltering pounding of music beneath her feet.

"Gotta go, there's a problem downstairs," she said into the phone and leapt to her feet. She didn't bother to put on her blazer to cover the fact she was carrying her .357, since she had it pulled from her shoulder holster and in her hand even as she flew down the stairs and into the theater below.

After all, her other girlfriend, Pamela Nelson—aka Storm—was dancing that day, and Brett was pretty damned sure it'd been Storm's scream she'd heard. So Brett leapt down the stairs, past Ted, yelling, "Turn on the goddamned lights!" and raced through the box office and into the auditorium.

Brett was barely through the door before she saw the last of the patrons racing out the back door. They didn't want to get involved in anything. They were like most of the men who came to the Paradise Theater—slimy. Indulging in porn and dancers on the side. They didn't want to be around if the cops showed. They wanted no proof that they'd ever been there, and police statements tended to be rather incriminating testaments as to one's whereabouts.

"Brett!" Storm screamed, as the lights flickered on. Brett had the drop on Storm's attackers, since her eyes hadn't yet adjusted to the darkness. She moved Storm into her left arm so she could clearly assess the situation and have her gun hand free. It didn't take long to determine the source of the problem.

"Stay where you are!" Brett ordered, pointing the gun at the two guys coming up the aisle toward her and Storm. Now she shoved Storm fully behind her. And then her brain registered who, exactly, they were.

"Ah, look, it's little what's-her-name," Matthew said, his thumbs in his pockets as he strode toward Brett and Storm. "Yo, Lukey, didn't they finally give her a name?"

"Yeah, Matt, they did. I think her name's Brett now," Luke said, coming up behind Matt.

"Ah, yeah, dude, little Brett. How I know her so well and all that, dude." He leered at Brett, then said to Storm, "She likes it when you force her. Make her do what you want."

"Leave, now," Brett said. She was covered in a cold chill, and every inch of her was shaking. She couldn't believe she was still able to aim at two of the six brothers she'd tried to forget existed.

Matt came right up to Brett, until her gun was dead-flat against the center of his chest. Then he brought his hand up and used it to push her hand down so her gun pointed harmlessly at the ground. "Whazzup, lil' sis?" he said, adjusting himself. "We was just acquaintin' ourselves with your friend here."

"Yeah, what'd that guy say her name was?" Luke said, reaching out to grab Storm from behind Brett. "Storm? Well, she's *baby* to me."

"No," Brett said, almost under her breath. Finally. Years too late.

"Oh, yeah, you got good taste these days, lil' sis," Matt said as he and Luke moved Storm between them. Brett was frozen.

"Oh, God, please, Brett, do something!" Storm said. Her back was against Brett's front. Brett's back was against the door, her gun still hanging uselessly next to her. Matthew ran a finger along the top of Storm's lacy black bra, while Luke ran his hand up the outside of her thigh.

"You 'spect lil' sis to do jack?" Luke said. Storm was between them as they pressed into her.

"She never did before," Matthew said, licking Storm's earlobe.

"Don't worry, little 'un, we'll get to you next."

"She'll just be happy if we just ignore her." Matt reached up to cup Storm's breasts.

"But it shore is nice to know she's doin' so great for herself," Luke said. "Warms our hearts and all."

"No." Brett hadn't seen any of her family since she'd walked out of the house to go to college. She never thought she'd see any of them ever again.

"Yo, did bitch say somethin'?" Matt said.

"Take your hands off her," Brett said, still pressed against the door. It was more of a whisper than a command, but it was the first time she'd really stood up against them.

"Didja say something, *baby*?" Matt said to Brett. "We ain't payin' 'nuff attention to ya? Is that it?" He took her gun from her and stuffed it into the back of his jeans. Then he pressed her up against the door. "Lil' sis miss me?" he whispered in her ear.

"No!" Storm said, pushing Luke away from her.

"If either of you motherfuckers think I won't shoot, you're even stupider than I imagined," Rick DeSilva said, coming in from the parking lot via the back door of the auditorium. He had his gun up and out. "Don't try to draw. Don't try shit. These women are important to me. More important than either of you are to anybody. And hey, what I say matters more than anything you two fucking morons might, 'cause I pay off half the police department. Monthly." He was talking as he moved up the aisle toward Brett and Storm and Brett's brothers. "I could drop your dirty, worthless carcasses on their fuckin' front porch and they'd ignore 'em if I told 'em to."

Matthew quickly turned about, pulling Brett's .357 from the back of his jeans.

Rick shot him in the thigh.

Matthew dropped the gun as he thudded to the floor, screaming. It went skittering to Rick, who picked it up. "That was fun. Anymore goddamned brilliant fucking ideas? Either of you? *Bueller?*" Rick kicked Brett's gun up to her. "Take it. It's yours. Never, ever, let anybody take it from you like that again. I expect more from you." He leaned down over Matthew. "By the way, I ain't never heard Brett scream like such a little girly girl. Ever. But one fuckin' shot and you're screaming like the bitch you are."

Chapter One
October 25

It was like a little people-locomotive going in and out of her house: Randi, Ski, Rowan and Allie. Each walking out carrying a box of something. Then they'd turn around, come back in and walk back out carrying more stuff. Always in the same order: Randi, Ski, Rowan and Allie.

"I don't see why you're the one moving out," Randi said, yet again passing by Brett, who was sitting on the couch, watching sports on TV. "Don't you *both* own this place?"

"Yes, we both own it," Allie said, "but Brett won't move out, and I won't—can't—continue living with her. Not after what she's done." With this, Allie stopped walking and stared at Brett. Fortunately, she was the last in line, so there was no sit-com-ish routine of folks bumping into each other.

"I screwed up," Brett said, not standing, not looking away from the television, not looking toward anyone. But she was painfully aware of every move Allie made. "I already admitted that. And I also told you it won't happen again."

"But how many times has it already happened?" Allie said. "This is just the first time I've actually caught you, and I'm sure it's not the only time you've fucked around on me."

Brett jumped to her feet. "So then what do you want from me? You seem to have all the answers already, but tell me this—what can I do to make it right?"

"I don't know you can," Allie said.

"You got your warning years ago," Randi said, coming back into the house, now empty-handed. "When you cheated on Allie with Storm."

"That wasn't cheating," Brett said. "I never promised monogamy."

"Oh, don't go changing your story all around now," Randi said. "You've always said what you did was wrong."

"Yes, because I should have been clear about it," Brett said.

"I was just a kid then, you bastard," Allie said. "I *trusted* you."

"Allie, honey," Brett said, approaching her. "I said I was sorry then. I'm still sorry. Now."

"But you did it again! You fucker, you did it *again!*" Allie screamed, pounding on Brett's chest.

Brett wrapped her arms around her and pulled Allie to her. She rocked Allie gently in her arms. "Shh, baby, shh." She ran her fingers over and through Allie's long, blond, silky locks.

"Don't engage, Allie," Randi said, standing behind Allie, her arms crossed in front of her. "Don't listen to her, don't talk with her, don't touch her."

"Get out of here, Randi," Brett said.

"No," Randi said. "Allie asked us to be here, to help, and unless she tells us to leave, we won't."

"You know nothing about this," Brett said. "What do you know about longevity? About sticking with the same woman for any real length of time? What's the longest you've been with anyone, huh? A few months, maybe? Do you have any idea how long Allie and I have been together? How many years?"

"But how many of those have you been faithful for?" Allie said, pulling away from Brett. "We've been together what? On then off then on again . . . A decade maybe? During all that time, have you *ever* been faithful?"

"Yes, damnit, yes, I have!"

"For how long? All at once? What's the longest you've ever been faithful for?"

"Years, baby, years. You would not believe how many times I've turned down temptation—how many times I've said no."

"Do you always say *baby* when you lie?" Ski asked from behind Allie and Randi. "Back up in Lansing, when we first met, you hit on me."

"The first time we met, Allie was with me and you called me a liar," Brett said. "Then I did whatever I had to to make sure you didn't arrest me. I did whatever I needed to to find the truth. To discover reality. You wanted to arrest me for murder, and I had to play you until I figured out who killed Chuck."

"So are you saying those two girls from the bar are the only ones?" Randi asked.

"Who's asking the questions here?" Brett asked. "Who's in charge?"

"Answer the question, don't sidestep," Ski said.

"Who's in charge?" Brett repeated.

"Shit," Allie said. "How many have there been?"

Brett realized she probably shouldn't lie anymore. "A few."

"A few *dozen*?" Randi asked, stepping forward.

"No! Just a few!"

"More or less than a dozen?" Ski asked.

"Less. Definitely less. Far less."

"Who?" Allie asked. "Tell me who!"

"Erika, Amber . . ." Brett trailed off, only naming the two women who had openly implicated her. She'd had a threesome

7

with them, and later on, Erika'd walked right up to Allie in a bar and told her what a great fuck Brett was.

"Fine," Allie said. "Be like that. For all I know, you've even screwed a ghost."

"What the hell are you talking about?" Brett asked.

"You know who I'm talking about," Allie said. "You said she haunted you. You saw her. Was that all you did?"

"Um," Ski said. "Allie, are you okay?"

"Yes, I'm fine. I'm remembering about the first time, after we got back together, that I thought Brett was cheating on me."

"So you're not gonna suspect me of screwing with Maddy or Leisa," Brett said. "Just a ghost, eh?"

"I watch you and Maddy, and Leisa, and there's nothing there," Allie said. She paused, staring at Brett. "Not like there was with . . . how you were . . . with . . . Her." She paused again, still staring at Brett. Then she glanced around the room, charged into Brett's office and stared at the walls, at the pictures Brett hung there. "Oh, God, Brett, tell me you didn't. Tell me you didn't."

Rowan, Ski, Randi and Brett all charged into the study behind Allie.

"Who?" Ski asked.

"Becky, Kathy, Pamela, Erika, Amber, Sarah, Jamie, Jessie— who haven't you screwed, Brett?"

"Who the hell are Jamie and Jessie?" Brett asked, then, to Allie's glare, added, "Becky, Sarah—hell, half the women on your list. More than!"

"So how do you want to make this work, huh?" Allie asked. "How are we gonna make us even? Huh, Brett?"

"I. Don't. Know."

"How 'bout we become mutually nonmonogamous, huh?" Allie turned toward Randi, as if about to grab her, but then glanced at Ski. "So how 'bout I hook it up with Rowan here, then, huh?" she said, then grabbed Rowan and kissed her, with both an arm and a leg flung about her.

Rowan almost pushed Allie away, but instead pulled her into her arms. And let her hands flow freely over Allie's nubile body. Brett leapt forward to yank Allie from Rowan's grasp. "What the fuck do you think you're doing?"

"Whatever I want," Allie said. "Just like you've been doing all along. What's good for the goose is good for the gander, isn't it?"

"So you're leaving me for Rowan, is that it?"

"No. I'm leaving you. Period."

Chapter Two

"Watch out behind you! He's coming after you!" Frankie yelled at Brett. "Kill that old bitch, then blast your way into that house!"

"This one?" Brett said, bouncing on her heels, her gaze cutting a swath right and left as she blew people out of the way while she ran to the house. She didn't think about those she killed; she killed mercilessly. They deserved to die, after all. They died and she lived. And that was what mattered.

"No! No!" Frankie yelled. "Not the clock tower! You'll get trapped up there and blown away!"

"Well, where the fuck is the goddamned house?" Her hands were shaking and her thumbs were on the triggers. She was ready to kill without thought, without remorse. Not that any was needed with these *people*.

"Jump down and run to your right! Goddamnit, Brett—run!

You're gonna get yourself killed!"

"Well, what the fuck is new? Where the fuck am I going?" Brett yelled. "Where's the goddamned house?"

"Use your knife! Use your knife!"

Brett slashed the guy coming at her from the left—slashed him, stabbed him, then saw the house and ran into it, barricading the door behind her.

"Quick, run over to that dresser under the stairs and grab the ammo there, grab the shotgun—"

"I got it, dude—is that a hand grenade?"

"Yes!"

Brett grabbed the shotgun and hand grenade, then ran upstairs, where she discovered a lot of zombie-like people coming in through the windows. She shot and cut 'em all up, slashing out and blowing their brains out.

"Dinner's ready!" Kurt yelled.

"I hate zombies," Brett said.

"They're not zombies. Don't use up all your shotgun ammo," Frankie said. "You need that for the bigger crowds."

"Okay, okay, but—shit! Does that guy have a fuckin' chainsaw?"

"Yes," Kurt said, coming into the room. "And he's chopped your head off, so now you're dead and it's time to come to dinner."

"Damnit," Brett said, staring at the TV screen.

"I swear to God," Kurt said. "I keep regretting I ever bought that thing for Frankie." He put plates down in front of Frankie and Brett, handed Brett a Miller Lite and Frankie a Faygo root beer in a beer mug.

"Thanks, honey," Frankie said.

Brett looked suspiciously at her grilled chicken, linguini and asparagus.

"Try it, you'll like it," Kurt said.

Brett did and did.

11

"It's all in how you cook it. Why do I keep having to teach you brutes that good, healthy food can taste really, really good?" Kurt said.

Brett leaned over her plate and glowered at Kurt as she cut up her food and sent it into her mouth in a steady flow. "So you bought Frankie the Wii?" she said, pronouncing *Wii* like it's supposed to be said: *Whee*. Or *we*.

"Kurt thought it'd be good for me to get some of my aggressiveness out with that. Y'know, kinda like some sort of anger management," Frankie said around mouthfuls of food.

Brett looked at their three plates and couldn't help but think of Goldilocks and the three bears, what with Frankie eating so very much and even she eating more than the petite Kurt. It was hard to believe Frankie and Kurt had already been together several years—even harder to believe that they'd lived together for more than a year now and that Kurt got away with being kinda bossy to both of them.

She woulda thought Frankie was the top, but she really wasn't so sure now that she knew them better.

"Well, it's the one video game where you don't merely sit on your ass twiddling your thumbs," Kurt said. "Plus I thought Dance Dance Revolution would be far more interesting than my latest Pilates tape." He winked at Brett. "Plus, it truly does work off any encroaching love handles."

"Hey," Frankie said. "I know you'd rather have me playing Resident Evil than *being* the resident evil."

"Yes, yes, virtually beating up the bad guys is far less likely to get you arrested than what you used to do," Kurt said. He put down the fork and knife he was using to eat European-style in order to stare across the table at the two compadres/criminals/coworkers/friends. "I just thought you might like some of the fun games instead of just the kill-kill-kill games. Anyway, let's get down to the more important matters of the night: Brett, how are you going to get Allie back?"

"I haven't got a fucking clue."

"You *are* going after her, though, right?"

"Of course I am. As far as I'm concerned, her little temper tantrum's just a temporary thing. And God knows, I ain't gonna lose her to some idiot like Rowan."

"Don't you understand?" Kurt asked. "It's not about you versus Rowan, or Randi, or anyone else. Allie needs you to be faithful to *her*, and be there for *her*, and help *her*."

"Hey, whenever she asks for my help, I'm there," Brett said.

"She is. C'mon, Kurt," Frankie said, "you know what hell Brett went through for Allie with that Rowan shit, and all that crap back in Alma—"

"Allie got me to pretend to be a high-school boy to help some of her friends, for fuck's sake," Brett filled in.

"—so you ask me," Frankie continued.

"Hold on," Kurt said. "You were a high school *boy?*"

Brett shrugged. "Well, yes."

"Did you make it with the head cheerleader?"

"Well, yes."

"Omigod, that is too much!" Kurt said.

"—Brett's done it all for her girl, except remain faithful," Frankie said.

"But that's all Allie wants!" Kurt said.

"No. If I'm being faithful, which now she thinks I never was, she'll complain about my job, or me beating people up or being unfeminist, whatever the hell that means."

"You need to do whatever you need to do," Kurt said, "to get Allie to forgive you, since you did, unquestionably, fuck up royally. I mean, not one but two women simultaneously?"

"Well, yeah, okay, I did that," Brett said.

"Like we ever thought you didn't," Kurt said.

"Coulda given me some credit," Brett said.

"Brett, that *was* the credit part," Frankie said.

"So what other games ya got?" Brett asked.

"There's this absolutely wacky and hilarious rabbit game," Kurt said, "and then there's Elebits and Mario and—"

"Wait'll you see The Godfather," Frankie said.

"You ox!" Kurt said. "I was surprised you didn't start with that, especially with how into all that Godfather stuff you are."

Frankie and Brett looked across the table at each other. "'Leave the gun, take the cannoli,'" they quoted in sync.

Chapter Three

November 8

Brett stood at the back of the main auditorium of the rebuilt Paradise Theater, her arms crossed in front of her as she watched Storm's little sister, Victoria Nelson, dance onstage. Victoria danced as Tempest, a name Brett'd given her, just like Brett had named Pamela Nelson Storm.

Brett turned and walked out, rapping on the cashier's bulletproof window en route. "I'm going home," she said. She was allowed to leave whenever she wanted. She owned half of it all now, after all.

Plus, Allie, the woman she'd started dating when she was dating Storm and had been with pretty much since then, was getting out of class soon.

And Brett wanted to see what she did, where she went and who she saw.

• • •

Brett sat a bit away from Rowan Abernathy's, watching through binoculars as Allie got home after classes. Brett knew where she'd been, since she knew her schedule, and, well, she'd been following her.

Just like she knew *where* she'd be.

She knew Allie hadn't been cheating on her, and she didn't think Allie'd hook up with someone right away either.

But then, Allie had known Rowan for years and years. So Brett felt pretty assured that nothing was going on between Rowan and Allie, and that Rowan was merely repaying Allie the kindness that Allie *and* Brett had shown her in proving her innocent of murder. Oh, and for saving her life, and Brett risking her own, while they were at it.

Brett waited in her car in the lot until Rowan got home and went inside to join Allie. Then she sneaked across the adjoining lawns, across the street and then the rest of the way to Rowan's, so she could peer in through the windows, watching what Allie and Rowan were up to.

Which wasn't much. At least, not yet.

She needed to get gone. She shouldn't be watching. She needed to win Allie back, not frighten her back into her arms. Or scare her from another lover.

But she loved her, and didn't want to be anywhere else, or look at anything else, than with her Allie.

She wanted to make sure she was safe. And happy. And whole.

Allie was the one really and truly good thing, the one thing that remained intact, about her life.

Even if she couldn't complete Allie, she needed to protect her.

And she needed to be absolutely certain that whatever she did, she didn't do a damned thing to push—or scare—Allie even further from her. She didn't want to make an unlivable situation worse.

• • •

16

Allie got out of her car and drew her coat around her. She couldn't help but shiver. It wasn't that she was cold, but instead, that she felt, yet again, as if someone was watching her.

She glanced around but saw no one. She thought about all of Brett's enemies, wondering if any of them could be watching her. Stalking her. Planning on killing her. She knew that every day with Brett was yet another day that being Brett's girlfriend could end up killing her, but being Brett's girlfriend still gave her a certain feeling of safety as well. But she wasn't that any longer.

And all of this was crazy making. She didn't want to think about all the people who would love to kill her just to hurt Brett. She didn't think they would actually kill her, especially not now that she and Brett were broken up, yet she hurried into Rowan's house, only stopping to quickly check the mailbox before unlocking the door and letting herself in. Rowan wasn't due home for about another hour yet, so Allie had a little time.

She kicked off her shoes at the door, put them into the shoe rack, then pulled off her sweater as she went back into the guest bedroom she was occupying. She put it into a drawer with her other sweaters and wondered what she'd ever seen in Brett.

Sure, yes, Brett was tall, dark, handsome and butch. But there was definitely a latent misogyny to her. Or, maybe, a self-misogyny of sorts. At the very least, deep inside, Brett had an unabiding hatred toward herself.

But she could touch Allie like she knew her better than Allie did herself. She touched Allie with such love and knowledge she could make Allie . . . open up. Let her touch and take her however she wanted. Brett was her Yoda.

She ignored the pics she'd kept from being tossed into storage in Rowan's basement, and went instead into Rowan's kitchen. Then her living room, peering out through the curtains for any untoward folks lurking about in the bushes. Or across the street. Or anywhere else.

She was definitely getting paranoid.

She'd always known, deep down inside, that Brett had never given up on her cheating ways. She'd always known Brett was playing around on her. And she'd always pulled the sheet around her *own* eyes. Because she loved Brett, and things were usually good with Brett, and, well, hell. Brett was a fucking fantastic lover.

But was that enough reason to let Brett get away with anything she wanted?

No.

It was just easier to go along with it all. To look the other way. But she couldn't help but wonder why Brett went with all these other women, what it was that Allie herself wasn't providing—what Brett got from these others that Allie couldn't give her.

Allie always knew there was some part of Brett—a rather large chunk—that Brett kept hidden from everyone. Likely even herself. Allie always thought if she gave and believed enough, she could finally get into that part of Brett and make everything all right.

But there wasn't enough to give, no matter what.

But still, Allie couldn't help but wonder what it was that had made Brett become who and what she was. Why she always had to keep seeking further and more and greater affirmation from so many around her.

She thought maybe she knew, but . . . she still yearned to cure Brett, because she loved her, yet. She wondered if maybe Brett's past was so bad that she couldn't help but jeopardize any love she might actually get, and subconsciously push anyone from her.

But Allie *did* have to watch out for herself, after all.

As soon as Allie and the rest of them were out of Brett's sight, on the infamous day of her move-out, Allie had apologized to Ski for almost kissing Randi. Ski had said it was no problem, but Allie didn't feel easy about it. She and Ski had run a rough road, and she didn't want to make it any worse.

Especially since she was pretty damned sure Ski knew Randi and Allie used to be involved, during the time when Allie and

Brett were broken up, many years before.

And Allie was terribly jealous of Ski and Randi since they were at the beginning of their voyage of love.

"*Looo-ooo-sy*, I'm home!" Rowan yelled a little while later, walking in the front door. She pushed off her shoes and took off her coat, putting both in the hall closet before going into the kitchen. "Whatever dinner is, it smells terrif."

"It's 'something's-beginning-to-smell-bad-in-the-refrigerator' night," Allie said, stirring things up in the pan. "It's almost ready. Why don't you go up, throw on your sweats, and come down and eat?"

"Okay. Be right back." Rowan quickly jogged up the stairs, disarmed, changed from her patrol uniform, and came back down. She was ever so much quicker at such things than Brett was. Of course, Brett usually didn't let Allie anywhere near the kitchen, except to clean up after the meal.

All because Allie'd burned a few meals back in their early days. One night of overcooked Tuna Helper and Brett would never forgive it. Not that Allie discouraged it much, since it was rather nice that Brett cooked so much.

But now Allie'd moved in with Rowan and realized that Lauren had always cooked for Rowan, so, unless they wanted to always eat out, she had to do the cooking herself. She was coming to like how Rowan enjoyed her meals. Her cooking. Her in the house.

When she was younger, she'd become a cop to help people. But then it'd all gone terribly wrong and she thought she'd shot and killed the wrong woman and . . . She still wanted to help people but had been unable to of late, except through helping Brett and Randi and her friends on various cases and with different situations.

Dinner wasn't much, but it *was* doing something for someone.

"So anything much happening at work lately?" Allie asked as

she dished out the rice with chicken and vegetable stir-fry onto their plates a few minutes later.

"Oh, God. Same-old same-old. Some B-and-Es, a bit of domestic violence, some teenagers wreaking random acts of vandalism. And some kid grabbing some handbags along Nine Mile. And you?"

"My women's studies classes seem to be filled with, well, a lot of angry women."

"Don't you think all women should be angry these days? All people with any sense of moral outrage, in fact? Anyone paying attention to the news? Or the government? Or paying attention at all?"

"Yes, but it's just . . . it seems as if it's better to not simply dwell on all the evil, but instead try to affect the parts you can affect. Don't just grumble and complain, but do something. Anything."

"Well, yes. That's why I do what I do, y'know? And c'mon, Al, we used to work together."

Brett saw Rowan come home, and she watched as she and Allie greeted each other. She saw the way Rowan ran up the stairs and hurried back down to rejoin Allie.

If she let them keep on living together, keep on being around each other so much, stay together like this, for very long at all, she knew they'd fall for each other.

And she had no intention of losing Allie to Rowan.

She sneaked back to her car when she saw Rowan reach over and put her hand on Allie's.

Brett wanted to go to an incredibly bad bar in an extremely bad neighborhood so she could get into a good fight and total someone. Hurt them beyond the telling of.

But she knew Allie didn't like her violent side and realized how much like Kurt Allie was, so she went to Tech Plaza at Twelve and Van Dyke. She remembered there used to be a Sanders there that was part sandwich counter, part bakery, part ice cream counter, part candy store. They had some good shit there.

Now she went to the Game Stop, hoping she could buy a Wii there.

She walked into the store and immediately felt dirty and wrong. There were geeks and young 'uns all around.

"Can I help you?" some prepubescent boy with a nametag that said his name was Alex asked when she walked in.

"Yeah, I was playing some games the other night at—"

"Hey, you got the Umbrella Chronicles?" a little boy asked.

"New on that wall, used on that one," Alex said.

"I'm looking for this thing called a Wii," Brett said when Alex looked back at her.

"Console, games or what?" Alex asked.

"How's the new Halo?" another kid asked Alex.

"Overrated," Alex said. He turned back to Brett.

"All of the above," Brett said.

"Call of Duty, Hitman or Assassin?" a boy barely out of his stroller asked Alex.

"Depends on what you want?"

"Something nasty and brutal."

"Then Manhunt, all the way."

If Brett was pissed off when she walked into the store, she was now about ready to go postal on the entire goddamned store. "I need a goddamned Wii and everything I need to make it work. And I need some good games where I get to kill a shitload of people."

"Do you have a guide for—" some kid asked Alex.

Brett grabbed Alex's arm and put a hand on her hip, so Alex could see her .357 in its shoulder harness. "Listen, fuckhead. I

21

want to spend a fuckload of money with you. I want to buy what-ever the fuck I need to to keep from going out and beating the fuck out of shitloads of assholes, got it?"

Alex was frozen in place.

"Alex, someone wants to know if he should get World of Warcraft or Tabula Rasa?"

Alex was still frozen in place, his gaze right on Brett's formi-dable gun.

The coworker, whose nametag identified her as Keri, grabbed Alex's arm and pushed him toward the other customers. "What can I help you with?" Keri was bright and perky, at most twenty-one, with long blond hair, green eyes and a nubile body.

And, as Brett looked at her, she realized Keri liked what she saw, from Brett's age, butchness and gun down to her leather, jeans and broad shoulders.

"I need to buy a Wii," Brett said. "And whatever else I need to make it work."

"Okay, we can do that," Keri said, leading Brett through the store and picking up items she put into Brett's arms. "You're lucky, we're one of the only retailers in this area that has Wiis in stock. You'll want a spare nunchuck and remote, plus this recharging station. Now, what sort of games are you interested in?"

Brett looked at Keri and thought of all the reindeer games they could play together. "There was some Godfather game a friend mentioned, and then there was some game we played at his place—I remember having to go through this, like, village and shoot up all these people—"

"Did it start at a farm?"

"Kinda, yeah."

"*Resident Evil*?"

"Yeah, that's it!"

"So tell me," Keri said, turning back to Brett. "Is there any-thing else you need . . . ?"

"You tell me."

"Well, why don't you tell me your name, first?"

"Brett, Brett Higgins."

"Well, Brett, tell me what you like, 'cause I'm sure you'd want more than you've got here."

Brett wanted to say she liked Keri. But tonight she was behaving, so she said, "I'm buying this so I don't go out to beat guys up."

"Okay, so you want to beat people up," Keri said, running her fingers up and down Brett's lapels.

Brett could only figure that Keri wasn't sure her signals had gotten through and so was upping the ampage on her flirtation. And God, Brett wanted to flirt back, and she wanted to take the girl to bed and . . . Instead, she said, "I'm getting this so I can be violent without hurting anyone." Then she took a deep breath and said, "Because my girlfriend doesn't like me beating up guys and all that shit."

"All righty then. So do you want sports ass-kicking, or other?"

"Other."

"Godfather, Resident Evil, Manhunt . . ." Keri gazed over the shelves. "You should try Zelda, and then maybe Call of Duty. How's that?"

"Got anything with swords?"

"Ooo, make sure to set her up with Rayman!" a guy—not Alex—said while rushing past her.

Keri gave Brett an up-and-down look. "No, I don't think so. But we can add in a Red Steel."

"Good, thanks." Brett took her armload of things up to the register and paid for them. She then escaped from the hell of geeks and prepubescents as quickly as possible.

Brett was in the parking lot, closing her trunk, when she felt a hand on her arm. She turned, pulling out her gun—

"Hey, just wanted to give you my e-mail address," Keri said, putting her hand on Brett's gun and guiding it back into the holster. She also tucked a card into Brett's pocket. "You like those games, or not, just e-mail me and I'll help you find some more of what you like." She ran her hand up and down Brett's arms suggestively, finally leaving them wrapped around Brett's shoulders.

Brett couldn't understand how this shit kept happening to her. It was all quite impossible. She ran a finger under Keri's nametag. "Keri, are you flirting with me?"

"Now why would I do that?" Keri asked, planting a hip on Brett's trunk.

"You tell me."

"You've got my name and e-mail," Keri said, walking back into the store.

Chapter Four
November 9

Brett stood at the back of the auditorium, watching as Tempest strode across the stage, moving to the music and taking control of her space. God, Tempest was *so* playing the dominatrix onstage these days!

Brett liked that Victoria only danced here, for her. She did it well, and consistently, and had quite quickly become a draw for the customers. That allowed Brett to justify booking her so much, not that she needed justification, but this way, it made sense and nobody could get angry with her over *preferential treatment*, or anything like that.

But as much as Brett liked watching Victoria dance onstage, because she entertained, and stripped and always kept doing new things, she could not watch her do lap dances.

Dancers at the Paradise paid the Paradise to dance there. It was a "stage fee." The dancers made their money doing lap dances—and at the Paradise, the dancers could decide how much they charged each customer for lap dances. Brett and Frankie also frequently looked away with regard to exactly what dancers offered for their fees. Brett was simply glad that the dancers she knew and liked didn't offer any special services, even for a lot of extra money.

Brett waived Victoria's stage fee because she was such a draw for the patrons, who paid fifteen dollars each to enter and could stay as long as they liked. In reality, she waived the $350-per-week fee as yet another way of helping Victoria out—without Allie knowing.

Brett had been able to support and help Victoria's older sister, Pamela (aka Storm), in less clandestine ways. Back then she hadn't been living, or commingling finances, with anyone.

Brett was walking back to her office, heading through the auditorium door, when she was stopped by a woman at the turnstile. "Brett? Brett Higgins?" the woman said.

Brett stopped, turned and looked at her. The woman wasn't bad looking, with long, dishwater-blond hair, a reasonably trim figure and slightly clouded blue eyes. It was as if someone had blurred the lens on a pretty, maybe even beautiful, woman. "Uh, yeah. What can I do for you?" The woman obviously wasn't the sort of dancer material Brett wanted.

"I'm hoping you can save me and my husband."

"Uh, yeah, okay, fine—and you are?"

"Laura."

"Laura who?"

"Do you really want to know?"

"Yes."

She looked around. Glancing about suspiciously, she said, "Here? Are you sure you want me to tell you *here*?"

"Yes." Brett knew that trying to hide something in this sort of environment was the best way to draw attention to it.

"I could tell you my maiden name, try to fool you with it, but

I won't. That'd just give you yet another reason to not listen to me, and not help me."

"So you gonna tell me already or what?"

"Higgins. My name is Laura Higgins. I'm your brother Luke's wife."

"Leave. Now."

"No, not until you hear what I have to say."

"Nope," Brett said, turning and walking into the box office. She closed each door behind her like she always did, but once she was out of sight, she ran up the stairs to her office.

She'd barely sat down to go over the contracts about leasing space in a nearby building to run an online erotic video shop when her phone rang. She picked it up. "Brett Higgins."

"Luke told me not to even try to contact you," Laura said hurriedly. "He said you wouldn't listen, for good reason—but he was proud of you and I don't know where else to turn! You're our only hope! We don't know why they're doing it or what they want!"

Brett slammed the receiver down and went back to reviewing the leasing contracts. Once she was assured they contained everything she wanted and nothing she didn't, she shredded the copies they'd asked her to sign, copied the originals, and signed and dated all versions thereof. People in this biz'd try anything, even making copies of one contract appear the same but actually be different.

She'd stopped by Rowan's on her way into work, to ensure Allie was still there. She'd watched Allie leave the house, get into her car and leave for class.

She did not, however, follow Allie to school. Where, even now, she should still be.

Brett knew she was stalking Allie and couldn't continue to keep such a watchful eye on her. She knew that if she did, Allie would eventually catch her at it. But it was like a sick addiction she couldn't cure herself of. And it made her feel like a total sleazeball asshole. As some TV show recently stated, stalking was the third most popular sport for men, behind luge.

She knew, deep down inside, that Allie would return to her. She knew it had happened before, and would happen again. Sometimes the best things came to those who looked the other way.

So she simply had to figure out how to look the other way now, and Allie would come back to her.

She put the contracts into envelopes with stamps and return-address stickers, then took them down and out to the nearest mailbox.

"He's proud of you, you know," Laura said, matching Brett stride for stride. "He saw how you overcame everything. It's only because of him that I knew to find you—and *where* to find you."

Brett dropped the mail down the slot, let the door close, then checked to make sure they had actually gone all the way down.

"He wouldn't come talk to you himself—he's too ashamed, because of the past and all. What he and the others did to you—"

Brett grabbed her, threw her against a wall, holding her off the ground with her forearm pressed against her throat. Laura weakly kicked her legs. "What do you know of it?"

"N-n-nothing," Laura gurgled out. She was gasping for breath. She brought up her hands to try to peel Brett's arm from her throat. "H-h-he just said . . ." She trailed off, her face becoming ever redder.

Brett let her down and released the pressure from her wind-pipe, letting Laura breathe, but still keeping her forearm against Laura's neck, ready to break it, or threaten her further. "What?"

Laura gulped great lungfuls of air. "He said he couldn't talk with you because of what he and his brothers did to you when you were younger. That's all."

"As far as I'm concerned, I'm an only child. An orphan. I have no family."

"I know it was bad, the way Luke just . . . glosses over it all.

But without you, you will soon have no family."

"Hmm. Now that's an idea I can get behind." Brett turned and walked back toward the theater.

"Somebody's killing all the Higginses they can find," Laura said, still a bit pink about the cheeks, as she practically ran to keep up with Brett. "So far they've killed your father, Matthew and John."

"Good for them. *Faster pussycat! Kill! Kill!* is all I gots to say about it."

Laura grabbed her arm as she opened the door to the Paradise. "Please, we've read about you in the papers—all the good things you've done, the killers you've helped put behind bars. Luke doesn't expect you to help, he doesn't think he deserves it, but he's trying to be a better person, really, he is. And he's doing it! But without your help, he might end up dead before he makes up for all the bad stuff he's done. I *know* I don't know all the bad he did, but he's a changed man these days—"

"Take your hand off me now, or else you're gonna lose it," Brett said, her voice coming from a deep dark place within herself.

Laura raced out her last words. "He's different ever since he went to prison, *again*, got paralyzed and got AIDS."

Brett whipped her switchblade out of her pocket. "So he got what was coming to him finally, eh?"

"Yes, he has," Laura said, quickly removing her hand from Brett, apparently in due respect for the size of Brett's blade. "So why not help prolong his torture? Every day he hates himself for the things he's done, and he knows he deserves all that he's going through. Why not help keep him like that? Puking in a wheelchair? He doesn't know I'm here, talking with you. He keeps saying he doesn't deserve forgiveness. He thinks he should be killed and put out of the misery he's in. But he's doing what he can to make up for all the crap he did before. And if he can do that, the rest can, too. Possibly. The rest of your family, that is. If you'll help them. If you'll let them. He's found the Lord, so why not the rest?"

Brett stared at her for a moment, unable to understand how anyone could ever come to her, begging for the lives of those who'd hurt her worse than any others ever could.

"I don't know what this person—this heathen—wants," Laura said, "but I know I want my husband safe. I don't know if it's just a killer, or what, but I do know that he hasn't asked for anything yet—no money or anything—and I also know that I have to do whatever I can to save the man I love. Surely you know something about this sort of love and devotion?"

"You do not know these people the way I do," Brett said. "They all deserve to die awful, horrible, evil deaths."

"Problems with another vendor?" Victoria said, walking up to them, returning to the theater after her lunch break. She stopped a stair beneath Brett and smiled up at her. Apparently she'd heard Brett's last statement.

"Then why not help," Laura said, "instead of letting him go quickly and easily to some sadistic serial killer?"

"Not so much, no," Brett said to Victoria, then looked at Laura. "Leave, now, 'cause I don't rightly give a good goddamn." When Laura pulled at her arm, she might've pushed her off, but she didn't want Victoria to see her striking, hitting or even pushing another woman.

"I met him when he was in rehab, getting off the drugs." Laura pressed on. "He found the easy way out after being in your father's house, going into organized crime, gangland stuff. He went to jail a few times, the last of which ended with him being paralyzed and HIV-positive. I was one of his nurses after. I worked at the clinic where he got off the dope. He wants to do better, be a better person, a better man."

"Oh, for fuck's sake, you're making it sound as if he was all born again and shit," Brett said.

"I know better than to say anything about anything like that to you," Laura said.

"I'm betting he didn't get AIDS getting gang-banged in the prison shower," Brett said. "He probably doped up or fucked anything that moved."

"Um, what's this all about?" Victoria asked.

Laura apparently saw some sort of an in with Victoria, so she said, "Somebody's killing off Brett's family."

"They've probably got a damned good reason," Brett said. "Or, well, maybe not. Maybe they just know 'em, 'cause that's reason enough."

Laura paused, then looked right at Victoria. "I've come asking her to help us find this person and stop him."

"Who?" Victoria asked.

"Whoever's killing her family," Laura said.

Brett again jumped in, this time with, "Okay, so, well, yeah, I got some friends in the Detroit P.D. Now gimme one fucking good reason I shouldn't call 'em and tell 'em to pretty much ignore these killings?"

"Please," Laura said, "all our money goes back into the community. Almost all of it—feeding the homeless, visiting the elderly, helping others. Luke's got some bad medical expenses, and between that and all the charitable work and donations, we can't afford special protection, or any expensive detectives or such. And the cops aren't paying much attention to us as it is. They don't think there's somebody out there killing your family. They think it's all acts of God or accidents or . . . other stuff."

"So you're coming to me for a freebie?" Brett said. "Is that it?"

"No," Victoria said, "she might not have the money to hire others, but you're better than them anyway. She's coming to you to save him *and* her." She looked to Laura for affirmation, and Laura nodded.

Brett grabbed Victoria by the elbow and led her into the dancers' dressing room. "Okay," Brett said. "You walked into the

31

middle of it."

"Yeah, I know, I missed the previews and all. I never cared much for those anyway. You hate your family, and somebody's killing them off, which would be good, usually. But one of your sisters-in-law or some such has come asking you for help."

"How'd you figure who she is?"

"I listened. Plus, you've never mentioned any sisters, besides which, she bears absolutely no resemblance to you. But because of the way she spoke, I'm kinda guessing she's related somehow. So, from what she was saying, I'm also guessing this all has to do with family."

"Yeah, so you ought to see right away why I'm not interested in helping. You got to be able to relate to this crap."

"Yeah, I do. You want them all dead. You want them all to suffer and die. Remember, my grandma knocked off her husband and hid his body. And I know I want to kill my father for what he did to me and to Pam. But then I'd always remember I killed him, and though there might be some glee there, I'd also have to live with the fact that I killed him."

"Babe, you got to know I've killed folks."

"But not in cold blood."

"Pretty much, yes. I have."

"Do you want to know one thing I've thought about so many times since finally finding you and starting to work here?" Victoria led Brett to the upstairs dressing area she'd claimed as her own.

"Not a clue here, babe."

Victoria turned and faced Brett. "I've thought about how if I asked you to, you'd make sure my father was dead. But he's family, so I can't do that. I love him, somehow, even though I hate him. Plus, I hope some day it all comes back to him and all that. Karmic retribution: He deserves to suffer, like I did, like Pammy did."

"Okay, so this affects me how?"

32

"You want your family to live to pay. Plus, from all I've heard, you can lord it over all of them. After all, you're like a multimillionaire now and all. Just imagine what it'll do to them to see who you've become—and then to have you come in and save the day. It'll kill 'em."

"Would you save your father if you could?"

"I can't say. But your dad's already dead. So it doesn't matter. But I will admit that I want him to suffer for eternity in a fiery hell."

"You actually want me to help those motherfuckers?"

"Yes. It'll help you keep your mind off the situation with Allie." Victoria reached up to brush her fingers through Brett's hair, then she cupped Brett's chin, leaned up and gently kissed her. "Plus I think it's what Allie would want."

Brett leaned down and kissed Victoria again, wrapping her arms around her and bringing her tight against her. "I love you. I loved your sister and I love you."

"But you also love Allie, too," Victoria said, pulling away. She took off her coat and draped it on a chair. "And you're miserable without her." She sat on a chair and raised one foot to Brett.

"Victoria, I'm sorry," Brett said, pulling off one stiletto-heeled boot and placing it on the floor under the dressing counter.

"I know." Victoria lifted her other foot, allowing Brett to pull off that boot as well. "You do realize you should've negotiated a nonmonotonous relationship from the start."

"Don't you mean—" Brett stopped herself, realizing that Victoria meant what she said.

Victoria stood and unbuttoned her blouse, and continued as if Brett hadn't said a word. "But you know, that wouldn't help you. You woulda gone mental as soon as you saw Allie with another butch." She turned, hung her blouse up on a hanger, then unzipped her tight jeans.

Brett's gaze was glued to Victoria's most excellent and sexy body the entire time. "I don't know why this happens to me. Why I end up falling in love with more than one woman at a time. I don't blame Allie for leaving me."

Victoria walked up to Brett, wearing only her black lacy bra and barely there thong. "I think what I mostly hold against you in all this mess is that you lost Allie not for someone you love, but for a quick fuck."

"It wasn't quick. And it wasn't just a fuck. Those two women wanted each other and needed me to make it happen."

"Are these the fairy tales you tell to put yourself to sleep at night?" Victoria picked up her skintight, one-piece leather jump-suit and slithered into it with the help of liberal applications of talcum powder.

"I don't know why I do what I do," Brett said, never once looking away from Victoria or her actions.

"I do."

"Care to fill me in, then?"

"You want to own, to conquer." Victoria slid the zipper up. "Plus, to put it bluntly and far too simply, a lot of survivors of sexual abuse either can't stand sex, or want it all the time."

"No, no, no." Brett grabbed Victoria. "Ever since your sister, I've loved every single woman I've slept with, up until Erika and Amber. But I do care for them, and we were all tossed together and it all just happened."

Victoria reached up and pulled Brett's head into her shoulder. "You've gone out of control, Brett. And now you have to let it all go."

Brett couldn't stop the tears as Victoria ran her fingers through her hair and ran calming hands down her back. She felt so right and safe in Victoria's arms, she couldn't help herself. "How do I go on from here? What do I do?"

"You keep busy. You try to move on," Victoria said as Brett dropped to her knees, moving with her, holding her all the way.

Brett wrapped her arms tightly around Victoria, burying her

face in Victoria's smooth, black locks. She unzipped the jumpsuit and pushed it off Victoria's shoulders, needing to feel skin, to smell the fresh, clean scent of her.

Victoria let her. "Brett, this will only postpone it. You need to deal with your family to deal with yourself."

"You sound like you're buying into all of their born-again, *praise-the-Lord* bullshit." Brett ripped herself from Victoria, rushing down the stairs. She stopped in the lower dressing room to gather herself.

"You wouldn't act this way if you didn't already know I was right," Victoria said, following Brett down the stairs.

Brett rubbed angrily at her eyes with her shirt sleeve. "No." She turned and ran toward her office, leaving the dressing room.

Allie was pissed. She was pissed that Brett had cheated on her. Repeatedly. She was pissed that her fellow students in her women's studies class were complete morons who didn't have a clue how the world really worked and couldn't understand that the women's movement in the Seventies practically imploded because all the women were totally judgmental about all the other women, instead of actually taking actions that might be supportive of each other and help change the world.

And she was increasingly sure that she wasn't just paranoid—that it wasn't people out to get Brett who were following her, but Brett herself. She hated that Brett was still getting to her.

She'd come to the Paradise to confront Brett on Brett's stalking of her. She had no proof of it, but she was pretty damned sure about it. And she was angry, angry at Brett and at life, and she just wanted to see Brett, but didn't want to admit it, so that added to her overall crankiness factor.

So when she'd walked in to hear the strange woman attacking Brett . . .

"They don't think there's somebody out there killing your family.

They think it's all acts of God or accidents or . . . other stuff."

"So you're coming to me for a freebie?" Brett said. "Is that it?"

"No," Victoria said, "she might not have the money to hire others, but you're better than them anyway. She's coming to you to save him and her."

. . . well, she couldn't help but want to know more—and Brett and Tempest's hasty retreat gave her just the chance to interrogate the unknown woman.

When she'd discovered the woman was Brett's sister-in-law . . .

"I'm sorry," Allie'd said, walking up to the strange woman just after Victoria and Brett had beaten a hasty retreat into the dancers' dressing rooms. "But I overheard part of that conversation."

"You're Allie, right?" the woman had said. "Brett's girlfriend, right?"

"Yes, but I don't know you," Allie said.

"I'm . . ." The woman looked down, obviously not wanting to answer the question.

"And I'm Brett's ex," Allie added. "I was a cop, and I couldn't help but overhear what you said about someone killing Brett's family?"

"I'm . . . I'm Laura, Brett's sister-in-law."

"And you came here because . . . ?" Allie'd heard just enough to have her interest piqued, and she wanted to know just why Laura was here. She knew there was no love lost between Brett and her family, so for a relative to have tracked her down—particularly a relative who seemed to know who Allie was, as well—meant something was going on. Something Allie might be able to use to her own advantage. She wanted—no, cross that, *needed*—more info. She might be able to use this to get Brett to do what she wanted for a change.

And right now, what Allie wanted was Brett to be spending far less time with Victoria.

"A lot of Brett's family's been getting killed lately," Laura said.

36

"Not *killed* killed, but dying under, well, under circumstances I'd call less than pristine. I'm not really buying that they just died. I think somebody's killing them all off."

"And you came here because . . . ?" Allie said, wanting something she could use.

"Luke and I have read about everything Brett's done," Laura said. "Everything *you* and Brett have done—"

"Her brother Luke?" Allie said. "Luke's your hubby?"

"Yes—but he's a changed man! He's nothing like he was before, and he's truly sad and repentant for most of what he's done in his life!" Laura was now practically clinging to Allie.

And Allie was sure that Laura'd pissed Brett off. And she could understand why.

But if she got Brett to look into whatever the hell Laura was on about, it would get Brett to stop following her. And Brett would be doing what she, Allie, wanted for a change. And that'd be nice.

Real nice.

And Allie wanted to be the one totally in control for a change.

So she found out more from Laura while she waited for Brett to reappear, and she listened to everything Laura had to say, and didn't want to admit that it sounded more and more like Laura was for real the more she heard—from the fact that the cops thought all the deaths were accidents and acts of God, to the fact that maybe someone was trying to kill off all the Higginses.

And when Brett reappeared, double-taking when she saw Allie talking with her sister-in-law—*Ha! How's it feel to have all the women in your life getting together and talking about you behind your back, Brett*—Allie was totally ready to deliver the punch line she'd come up with, one that Brett took like a punch to the face: "Yeah, this one thinks she can get away with anything, and deserves to, but can't do any forgiving herself. She holds a grudge. Even when she's guilty. And don't worry, if she tries to pull the Detroit P.D. off the case, have them give me a call. I carry more cachet with them regardless."

Brett heard Allie's words and took a deep breath, willing her breathing to even out. "Fine, will my investigating this make things better between us?" She heard the door behind her, the door to the dancers' dressing room, quickly snick open, then closed again. She figured Victoria was about to come after her, but realized Allie was there.

"Yes," Allie said, with a steely façade as she gazed at Brett. "In that it will give you less time to stalk me, and also maybe convince me to not take out a warrant against you, or any other sort of court order against you in regard to such matters."

Chapter Five

Brett sat back in her chair, her feet up on her windowsill. Today, right now, she was looking up at the bright blue sky above. She'd seen many bad things from these windows, stopped some of it and ignored other parts. Right now, she frankly didn't give a good goddamn.

She sipped her Laguvalin and lit another Marlboro Light off the Zippo Storm had given her oh, those many long years ago. She had quite a collection of Zippos, but she kept it at the office, in a drawer, and not on display, where just anyone could see it.

She heard the door at the base of the steps open then close. She heard steps coming up the stairs. It was amazing how individual footsteps could sound, and how even more especially individual they became when combined with a door opening and closing. People walked differently, climbed stairs differently, and opened and closed doors differently. She always knew who it was coming to visit her, even if all she knew was that she didn't know the person.

Brett held up the bottle in one hand, her glass in another. "Remind me again why I don't usually drink this stuff?"

Victoria, Tempest, took the bottle from her hand and glanced at it. "Because it tastes like dirty dirt." She poured another two fingers into Brett's glass, then went to the bar to get some ice to drop into the glass. Victoria dipped a finger into the Scotch and slipped it between her own lips. "I tend to agree."

"Good show?" Brett didn't look away from the blue sky and the lazily drifting fluffy white clouds.

"I got the hell out of there as soon as I could," Victoria said, taking the cigarettes and lighter from Brett to look at them. "I wanted to get back to you. Be with you." She studied the lighter for a moment. "I've changed my mind. I think you should let them die. Let them all die." She replaced the lighter in Brett's hand, wrapping her hand around both while doing so.

Brett took another sip of the Laguvalin. "Yeah, you're right. Dirty dirt. Normally I couldn't condone ice in good Scotch, but this is peat, so . . . yeah. Thanks. So why are you now changing your mind about what I should do?"

Brett knew Victoria went to her computer and saw what she had been looking at: an article about Luke and Laura Higgins's ministry. And she listened as Victoria paged back through to see the results of Brett's Googling of +"Luke Higgins" +"Laura Higgins." Further back-paging would reveal further Googling of other Higgins family members. It wouldn't take Victoria much to realize Brett had spent the past hour and a half Googling her family to find out as much as she could about them, finding obituaries and arrests, and all the crap about how Laura'd helped Luke turn his life around to help others find a way out of the gutter and make themselves into productive members of society. All while becoming Jim and Tammy Faye rich.

"Laura seemed to think that maybe there was a reason somebody's killin' 'em off." Brett pushed herself to her feet to wrap herself around Victoria from behind, spooning their bodies together. "I reckon that, if somebody's actually doin' it, they're doing it 'cause it's the right thing to do."

Victoria stiffened a moment before melting into Brett. "I was trying to do what was right, before. I was trying to help you. I set aside my feelings . . . my jealousy . . . toward Allie, to try to help you. I knew I wanted you—for myself—but was willing to help you back to her—for you. Because that's what I thought you wanted and needed."

"I'm not even sure somebody's killed any of them," Brett said. "Could be they're all just offing themselves Darwin style— through sheer stupidity." Brett ran her hands up Tempest, up her thighs. She flipped around, grabbed Tempest by the hips, and brought her up to ride her waist. Brett slammed Tempest into the wall, grinding her belt buckle into Tempest's cunt.

"No," Tempest said, pushing against Brett with her hands.

Brett grabbed both those hands in one of hers and held them against the wall over Tempest's head. She reached down to rip open the front of Tempest's bikini top, revealing her breasts.

"Stop!" Tempest said, writhing and squirming against Brett.

Brett ripped off Tempest's G-string, briefly cupping her cunt before going up to tweak one of her nipples.

"Please, Brett, no, stop!"

Brett suddenly looked at Victoria, then stopped and pulled away, releasing Victoria's arms and dropping her down to her feet. "I . . . sorry . . ."

"Brett—"

Brett ripped at her own hair. She wasn't *that* drunk. But it was still as if something was invading her brain. It was like one of those nights she couldn't sleep because she was too scared to. And not scared of anything in particular, but simply . . . afraid to sleep. Because. Because she was scared. Afraid. Couldn't do it. It was like something short-circuited in her brain.

She dropped to her knees, shaking from the inside out for what she almost did. Maybe she shoulda taken some sorta psych course in college, but it wasn't like anything else she'd taken during her BA in business had helped her any since, so why would that have actually helped, either?

Victoria wrapped her body around Brett's, cushioning her and comforting her. "It's okay. It's okay, baby," she repeated, over and over again. Victoria's arms, Allie's arms, femme arms, could help her more than any psych class ever could've.

Brett looked up at Victoria, suddenly feeling very much like a cornered and trapped animal and knowing she had to get out of there. "How would you know?" She clenched and unclenched her fists, pushing back against Victoria, pushing for her freedom. "It's not okay."

Victoria held her tighter.

"No," Brett said. "You only had a sister. You can't understand. It's not the same."

"Walk away from this while you still can."

"No, I can't. You started this—me going into it. I can't walk away now."

Brett still couldn't stand, couldn't regain her feet, but she knew where she was heading. She wasn't sure why, or where it would end up, but she knew she had to go there.

She wanted to hit Victoria, knowing it was because of Victoria that she was having to do this. But she couldn't hit her because . . . it was Wrong. She couldn't because that wasn't who she was.

And then a part of her brain stepped in, telling her she could still escape . . . but she knew she couldn't, not really.

There was never any escape.

"Brett, you've run away from yourself before. You changed your name and started a new life. You only came back to this one through your own choice."

"Well, that and evil cops and so-called friends and other badness." It was grounding to be back in the real world. To discuss things of the here and now, and get outside of the horror inside her own head.

"But the thing is, you're an adult now. You're a big, butch, bad-ass woman. You don't have to do anything you don't want to. You're in charge of your own life now and can do what you want. And that big-ass gun you carry pretty much guarantees nobody's gonna fuck with you or make you do anything you don't want to."

"Brett, what the fuck are you doing?" Frankie said, storming into her office and glaring at her and Victoria. "I just got done talking with Allie and Laura. You need to get on it yesterday."

Frankie and Brett had never disagreed or argued. The closest they'd ever come was to provide insight on each other's life and choices. "Why? To send whoever's doing 'em thank-you notes? I mean, fuck, if I coulda done in my fam when I was growing up, I sure as fuck woulda. The only reason I haven't done it in the past decade is that they're not worth the time or trouble—so why should I waste any time trying to save 'em?"

"To get Allie back, dude," Frankie said.

"I can't, Frankie."

"You've got to do this. You ain't got no choice."

"She can't," Victoria said, standing up and facing off with Frankie.

"Allie's family," Frankie said. "And you do anything for family. It's all about family."

"Not when it's *her* family," Victoria said, indicating Brett. "Or mine."

Frankie stared down at her, his arms crossed in front of his broad chest. "Then she should do it for Allie, 'cause Allie's her real family—one of the ones who matters."

"So yeah," Victoria said. "I'm only the parsley on the plate." She grabbed Frankie by the arm and pulled him to the door. "I was right there with you, Frankie. I was all with convincing Brett she had to get on this. I don't want Brett by default. I want her to come to me by herself. Of her own free will."

"Um, excuse me?" Brett said. "Right here? As in, hearing every word of this?"

"Yeah, so you should be hearing that you need to do what Allie's asking you to do," Frankie said.

"But doing *just* that *just* might destroy Brett," Victoria said.

"Still here!" Brett said. "And I haven't decided one way or the other yet, okay? Both of you?"

"Brett," Frankie said. "Listen to her—she's *happy* you finally got caught. She knows you're not gonna end up with one of those floozies from the bar. She wants to help break you and Allie up so she can make her move. Meanwhile, Allie wants you to do this so she knows you can forgive as much as you want to be forgiven."

"Okay, fine," Brett said to Frankie. "Then you help make it happen. Use your contacts to get full criminal histories on everyone in my family." She sat down at her computer, quickly typing in full names for all of her family so she could give it to him. "I can only get so much info off the Net, and I'm thinking all of my police contacts have probably dried up at this point."

"If it's Allie doing the asking, then she should be willing to help out," Victoria said.

"She was asking on behalf of Laura," Brett said. "And I want her involved as little as possible. Thus, Frankie." She sat staring at her monitor, trying to think of anyone else she should have looked into—any other possible perps. Or folks she needed info on to build a better, clearer picture of it all. But first she thought of the other abusers in her family, other relatives, and added those names to her list.

And then she thought about Marie.

And that was one thing—one woman—she didn't want to think about.

So she hit print and handed the sheet to Frankie. "You want

me on this, you gotta help, too. I have very few, if any, contacts left with the P.D., and I'm not about to burn them out by asking favors to help my fam."

"As well you shouldn't," Victoria said. She had her arms crossed in front of her, and not out of embarrassment of being so under-clothed in front of Frankie, since she well knew he was a full-on fag regardless of his appearance, but probably because she wasn't in with Brett helping her fam out. Not now.

"Fine," Frankie said. "I'll get it done."

Brett realized these two wouldn't leave her alone long enough to do what she needed to do. Plus, Frankie couldn't get her the info she needed until she released him to do so.

"Victoria," Brett said. "You have to get ready for the next show. You're working today, after all. Frankie, you need to get on that. And all this arguing ain't makin' a damned thing happen. So I'm gonna go home and do some research from there."

"So what are we supposed to do?" Frankie asked.

"Your jobs. What I told you to do. And leave me alone. I can work better from home on this." She grabbed the stacks of print-outs from her desk, loaded them into her briefcase, donned her leather trench and left.

Chapter Six

Brett pulled photo albums off their shelves. Pretty much, they started during her freshman year of college—and actually, all of college only took one album. She started collecting more photos after college, and then with Storm, and even more so with Allie.

She went down into the basement to go through some long-term storage boxes Allie'd stashed down there. Brett was pretty sure she'd had a few pics from her younger years that she'd kept, and she was thinking that maybe they'd help jostle her memory—remind her of things she'd rather forget. But she was willing to try to remember if it'd help her get Allie back.

At the very least, she had to make it *look* like she was trying to help. She had to put on a good show.

Fortunately, Allie was very thorough and organized. She'd labeled each of the boxes on all of the storage shelves—from her own early days, stuff she'd gotten from her parents, holiday ornaments, old bank statements, to . . . bingo! *Old Brett Stuff* was written in red on one box down on the bottom.

Brett stared at it for a moment. Then a moment more. Then she went upstairs to grab a Miller Lite, an ashtray and a pack of smokes. She went into her study, checked her e-mail, printed out the spreadsheet she'd sent herself (with gridlines), put it onto a clipboard and went back downstairs.

She wished she could've been the one to kill off her family. She would've loved to be capable of it when she was growing up.

Actually, there wasn't any reason for her not to do it, now that she could. It was what she ought to do.

She took a deep pull off her bottle and started slowly removing the boxes from on top of hers. Then she pulled out *Old Brett Stuff*, finished her beer, went upstairs, got two more, came back down, lit a cig and sat down with her clipboard and pen next to the box of doom.

She couldn't remember what she'd have saved from her life before college. She knew she'd saved the little button eyes off her Boo Boo Bearski, which her brother Matthew burned right in front of her.

But she'd thrown those away years ago, once she tossed in with Rick DeSilva and Frankie Lorenzini. Once she stepped out and above all that had gone before.

She was relieved when the first things she pulled out were her old college transcripts, plus a few grade reports from college, as well as some papers, a few random pictures (God, she barely remembered that roommate!), a notebook, a Michigan State University bumper sticker (she and some friends sometimes referred to her alma mater, MSU, as the school of Making Stuff Up), and then a little container of the sort that came from a bubble-gum machine. Normally, they'd have a little toy or stickers or something in it, but this one had a lock of golden hair.

"Brett!" Merry screamed, opening Brett's Christmas present to her.

It was a cheap little locket. Merry threw her arms around Brett's neck, throwing herself into Brett's arms and pulling them both to the ground. She fell on top of Brett.

Everything was foggy to Brett, looking back at it now, but she reckoned they were about nine years old.

"I need a pic of you to put in it," Merry said.
"I . . . I don't have one," Brett reluctantly said.
"Then I'll need some little bit of you!"
"What?"
"Oh, silly, I just need something to keep you close to me always!" Marie Higgins, Brett's first cousin, whom she alone referred to as Merry, said, looking around to find a pair of scissors. She quickly snipped off a bit of Brett's hair, enclosed it in the locket and put it around her neck. "Now you'll always be close to my heart."
Brett was quite pleased with Marie's gift of comic books. By the next time they saw each other, though, Brett's brothers had stolen and ruined the books. But Merry pressed a small capsule into Brett's hand. "So you always have a part of me, too," she'd said.
When Brett opened the container later, the hair felt like the silk that was on top of Merry's head, and it smelled like Merry herself. Brett almost never opened the container, wanting to be able to fully savor and treasure it all forever.

Brett now opened the capsule, carefully fingering the still silky strands. She lowered her head to take a whiff of the hair, which even yet kept the slightest bit of Merry's essence. Brett breathed again from the hair, not sure how much of it was the actual scent of the hair and how much was her memory, but these strands smelled like Merry to her, and made her think about her cousin. And remember every moment she'd ever spent with her.

She stared down at her printed-out spreadsheet. And she

wrote down every member of Merry's family, and everyone who might've held a grudge against them for what happened to her.

Thinking about the grudge aspect got Brett going on the blame game. She started writing down more names to look into and research.

And even as she wrote down the names and went upstairs to Google some more, she remembered the last time she saw Merry: Brett was managing the Paradise Theater, and Merry came in to audition to be a dancer there. She was an emaciated, drug-addicted prostitute.

Brett gave Storm money to feed Merry, and some to give her. To preferably not spend on drugs.

Brett hadn't been able to save Merry. Hadn't been able to save so many like her. She hadn't been able to save Eliza, up in Alma, or . . .

She Googled and printed. Newspaper articles. Stuff about arrests. Obituaries. Of folks she was related to that Laura hadn't mentioned.

She researched herself, her life, her relatives, and all that online. It seemed as if Laura had been telling the truth, but hadn't told quite all of it. More relatives were dead than Laura mentioned.

And Brett still wasn't sure if Laura and Luke were on the up-and-up about what they were doing. She had no love of religious sorts, and apparently her bro Luke had gotten religion somewhere along the way. He walked up to death's door, and was now a minister.

And Brett didn't trust no ministers. Nobody who said they could make it all better was telling the truth, far as she was concerned.

So she started trying to debunk their ministry . . . Because not only was that a sensible line of action, but also it kept her from that box in the basement, which was almost throbbing with the potential of untold horrors.

And only Brett's quickly becoming inebriated mind could come up with such a line.

Brett leaned back into Merry's arms. "I've missed you," Merry whispered into her ear.

They were thirteen, and Brett had been studying at her desk, trying to pay attention to her advanced algebra, because she knew her cousin was about to be there. Her cousin was coming, and she missed her so much and wanted to see that she was all right, okay, so much. So badly, so much.

They didn't get to see each other nearly enough, and each time they were apart for any length of time, Brett worried about her dear, sweet, Merry. She was tougher and stronger than Merry, she could take care of herself. And even when she couldn't, she wouldn't let Merry know—because she could deal with it all better than Merry could.

She knew how to leave her body and her life and go somewhere else in her mind.

But now Merry was with her, sitting behind her on her chair. Brett put her hands on Merry's, enjoying the warmth and pulling her closer to her.

"So what is this?" Merry asked, her breath again tickling Brett's ear as she looked over her shoulder to see what Brett was studying. "Ooo, God, it looks really mathish."

"It's algebra," Brett said, turning her head to look at Merry. "Holy shit!" she yelled, twisting her entire body around so she could face Merry and take her face in her hands. She ran her thumbs lightly over the bruised and swelling area that covered nearly half of Merry's face.

"Please," Merry said, closing her eyes and taking Brett's hands into her own, "calm down. It's all right."

"It's not all right—who did this?"

"Brett, we both know this isn't the first time, and it's happened to both of us. And it'll happen again. To both of us. Right now I want to be with you. That's what'll help me get through this and the next time this happens. Hold me and then let's have fun and laugh and joke

around like we always do. Let's be us and let everything else go and forget about everything else." Merry buried her face in Brett's shoulder, and Brett pulled her so close Merry's thighs, which were straddling the chair, were now on top of Brett's, which were also straddling the chair.

Brett caressed Merry's hair with her cheek, gently stroking her back and holding her tight. "So . . ." She wanted to find out who did this, but knew Merry was right: Their best chance of making it out alive was to help each other. "The courtroom was dead silent when the prosecuting attorney confronted Santa. 'Do you admit, sir, that you, in front of not only this woman's children but an entire mall full of children, called my client a 'Ho,' not once, not twice, but three times?'"

There was a moment, then Merry buried her face deeper into Brett's shoulder, and then Brett felt her trembling and shaking and she hated herself for making Merry cry, but then Merry pulled away, laughing. "You can always make me laugh, Brett. Maybe that's why I love you like I do."

She really didn't mean anything with those words, Brett knew. Not then.

Unless . . . maybe she did. After all, they'd both had to grow up so quickly. Actually, neither of them had a childhood at all.

A year later, when they were fourteen, it was a summertime barbecue at the Higgins home, which meant lots of drinking and yelling and whatever else. Pretty much, Merry and Brett realized young that it was in their best interests to become scarce at such times.

Yes, there were other children there, but at some point Brett and Merry, who were the same age, realized they'd be lucky to make it out themselves. They couldn't help anyone else.

Brett and Merry knew the best routes to take to get up past Eight Mile safely. They'd spend the day walking all over, miles and miles. They'd try to get back to Brett's after everyone passed out. Inside the house was scarier than outside, even in such bad parts of a bad city.

They joked and laughed throughout the day, holding hands for most of the time. It was something they'd always done, but that day, Brett noticed folks noticing them touching—especially as they walked through Ferndale. Ferndale, which Brett would later know as a gay mecca . . .

And that was the night . . .

Brett's thoughts were interrupted by a persistent pounding. On the front door. She pulled herself out of her reverie to answer it. Knowing most of her friends, they'd break in if she didn't answer. So she answered.

Without looking through the peephole first. Without knowing who it was.

"You've been crying," Victoria said, stepping over the threshold and rubbing her thumb over the tearstains on Brett's cheeks.

Brett pulled angrily away from her, turning her back on Victoria as she went to grab another beer.

Victoria closed the door behind her, took off her coat, draped it over one of the kitchen chairs and went to Brett.

"You want something to drink? Eat?" Brett asked.

"Whatever you're having."

Brett quickly twisted off the caps on both bottles and handed one to Victoria. "So what's up?"

"I wanted to see how you were doing."

"I'm fine. Anything else?"

"You're not fine. C'mon, talk to me," Victoria said, taking one of Brett's hands and pulling her along to the living room sofa.

Brett stopped. "I'm fine. Copacetic. Five by five, even."

"I don't understand half of what you said, but what I do know is that every word was a goddamned lie. If you're going to make it through this, you're going to have to talk about it. So sit your goddamned ass down and talk to me—I am the only person you know who will not only listen, but will also understand." Victoria ran her hand up Brett's arm and cupped her cheek. "What's going on? The truth."

Brett pulled away. She wanted to talk, but couldn't. She'd

never shared any of this with anyone else. The closest she'd come was with Storm. But now Storm was gone. Allie only knew the barest of information about it all. She knew the icing.

"Talk to me."

Brett didn't look at her. "I've been going through old files and records and pics trying to brainstorm who might be responsible, who might be next, and all of that. That is, if there is someone responsible, and not just my relatives being their normal, self-centered, bastard idiot selves."

"Oh, God, Brett," Victoria said, guiding Brett down onto the couch and bringing her head into her lap.

Brett tried to resist, but there was so very little of her left. When she felt Victoria's fingers running through her hair, so comfortingly, she couldn't hold back any longer: She began crying. She buried her head, her face, in Victoria's lap and cried.

She and Merry climbed up the side of the house and in through Brett's bedroom window. As soon as Brett locked the door with a chair pressed up under the doorknob, they both quickly took off their shoes, socks and jeans and climbed into Brett's twin bed together. Merry tossed her leg over Brett's, curling as closely into Brett as she could.

Brett ran her fingers along Merry's spine. They'd slept like this whenever they could for years, but now they were . . . fitting together differently. Brett had been noticing all day how Merry's body had changed, and every time she did so, it felt as if all her nerve endings were on edge.

"Mmmm, that feels good," Merry said, pushing in closer to Brett.

Brett was lightly tapping her fingers up and down Merry's back, enjoying the feel of Merry's skin under her fingertips. And now she went a bit lower, and then lower still and then she let her hand gently, and briefly, cup Merry's butt. The next time she let herself linger there a moment longer. Then she went down farther to feel the top of Merry's thigh, finger the elastic of her panties . . .

She thought Merry was asleep. And she loved the feel of her body, the softness of her skin, the scent of her and how they fit together.

But then Merry pushed herself up onto her forearms, so she could look down at Brett. She flipped her long blond hair over her shoulder. "Brett," she said.

"I'm sorry," Brett whispered, forcing her hand from Merry's body and onto the bed next to them. She allowed her other arm to remain holding Merry to her. She desperately hoped she hadn't screwed up everything between them.

"No. Don't be sorry." Merry looked down at her with somber eyes. "I like it when you touch me." She raised herself up onto her knees and pulled her tank top off. Brett lost her breath at the first sight she'd ever had in real life of real breasts. They were small, but she couldn't help but look at them and want to touch them. But Merry lay back down on top of her. "Sorry. I just want . . . I want to be as close to you as possible. I want to feel you against me."

Brett let her hands wander over Merry's bare back, caressing her skin, feeling her closeness. "Merry," she said, raising her head to kiss Merry's neck gently.

"I like that you call me that. Nobody else does."

"I'm glad."

Merry pushed herself up again, looking down at Brett by the light of the full moon. Her hair cascaded around them like a nightshade. She leaned down and touched her lips to Brett's. After a few minutes of their lips touching and caressing, she slipped her tongue out to lick lightly along Brett's lip.

Brett's tongue met hers. And they were both gentle and hesitant and tentative.

"You know it all already," Brett said into Victoria's lap.

"I think I know some of it. But I'm not sure. And you need to talk about it. And I know enough to guess about it, and I'm the one person you know who can relate."

"Yeah," Brett said, reaching to grab several tissues from the box on the coffee table. "Like anybody'd ever try to pull that shit on Frankie. And Allie . . ." She burst into a fresh round of tears.

"It's okay."

"She doesn't know."

"I know."

Brett tried to stop thinking about the past—especially about Merry. Which brought about a new round of body-wrenching sobs.

Victoria gently touched her hair, ran a hand down her arm, her back, all the while talking. "It's okay, breathe. Just breathe. You can tell me anything, you know, and I won't think any less of you. You saved me and my sister."

"I couldn't save Storm."

"But you tried. And she lived years longer than she would have without you. And I think, for the first time in her life, she was happy. Really happy with you."

"And she died when I was in another woman's bed." Brett had been with Allie when Storm was killed.

"I know Brett, and I still love you, and she did, too."

"Why'd Matthew have to kill Boo Boo?"

"Left field, yes. What are you talking about?"

"I don't want to talk about how I screwed your sister over, so I was attempting a clever distraction toward the one real toy I had growing up: My bear. Boo Boo Bearski. My brother torched Boo Boo while I watched." Brett kept her face buried in Victoria's lap. Victoria's fingers running through her hair felt so good. Right up until she heard the front door open.

"I knew it," Allie said, walking in the front door. "I knew there was something between you two."

Brett sprang to her feet. "Allie, wait!" She hadn't even heard Allie's key in the lock—had she even locked it?

"What? So you can create yet another story?" Allie asked, stopping on her way back out to turn and confront Brett.

"No. Nothing was going on here. Victoria was being a friend. A good friend. She was . . ." Brett faltered, unsure of what to say.

"I was worried about her," Victoria said. "She seemed upset earlier today. So I stopped by on my way home, like any good friend would." She picked up her coat and headed for the door, stopping to say quite pointedly to Allie, "I'll go now that you're here."

"No, Victoria, wait," Brett said, taking her hand. "Thank you."

Allie watched as Victoria got into her car and drove off. Then she turned back to Brett. "So are you sleeping with her, too?"

"She was being a friend. I was looking into Luke and Laura earlier, and I got home, and looked into . . . found . . . that box in the basement. Which brought back memories and—"

"Brett, could you at least try to speak English?"

"Allie, all of today has been about fucked-up fucking bad-ass memories. It's not been a happy day, and Victoria saw it coming. She stopped by tonight to try to help me, because she knew you wouldn't be here."

"Well, I am here."

"Now. For how long?"

"What is it you need help with? What is it that I can do for you?"

"Why the fuck did you come by here tonight?" Brett asked, going to the fridge for another beer. "To rub it all in? To scare Victoria off? To try to catch me misbehaving again? Why?" She turned to face off with Allie.

"Part of this house is still mine. And I remembered the stuff, the boxes, in the basement."

"So get 'em and get gone."

"Are you kicking me out?"

"Allie, do you have any idea what seeing Laura today, and having her ask me to help my family, did to me?"

"No. I don't. Because you don't tell me about this stuff. You don't talk to me about it."

"Allie . . . sometimes this crap is too much. I *can't* talk about it."

"But you *can* talk with *Victoria* about it."

"No. She understands. She knows without me saying."

"So because I'm not somehow telepathic I'm not worthy?"

"Allie. It's not that. She understands because she's been through it, too."

"So tell me so I can understand as well."

"It's not something I can tell. I can't talk about it, Allie. Honey."

"Is that the motto of our relationship? 'I can't talk about it'?"

"Well as far as mottos go, it's better than 'Some people don't look good in Santa hats.'"

They were facing off, mere inches from each other. "So is now when you grab me and throw me against some wall, fucking me senseless to change the subject?" Allie asked.

"I was thinking about it, yes," Brett admitted.

"Ain't gonna happen," Allie said, backing away from Brett.

"To talk about it means that I need to think about it, and I'm thinking about it all more than I should by just looking at stuff." Brett felt like breaking down into tears again. But she didn't want to do it again. Especially since . . . well . . . She couldn't. Not around Allie. Especially not now.

"Fine. Then I'll be by tomorrow night for those boxes. Does that work for you?" It wasn't a question.

"We can load them up now if you'd like."

"Tomorrow. After class. About seven," Allie said, leaving.

Chapter Seven
November 10

The next morning, Brett drove past Rowan's to check up on Allie, then went into work for two hours. Just long enough to apologize to Victoria for the way Allie'd been the night before, take care of a bit of work and tell Frankie she'd be out the rest of the day.

Then she drove to the old neighborhood. She drove by her old high school. She cruised the streets of her old neighborhood, feeling every moment as if someone was following her, but knowing it was just that she was in a place she no longer belonged and had never wanted to be—it was as if the evilness of her past and all she'd been through was following her around, like some sorta mangy mutt. Except that'd be an insult to mangy mutts the world over.

She parked across the street from the house she grew up in. And she sat there and stared at it. Loathing it and everything that'd happened in it.

It seemed right that she felt lousy with her hangover as she sat looking at the house she'd experienced so much horror in. And it hadn't changed one bit. It was as run-down looking and dirty as always, with cracked walkways and peeling paint.

She wondered if her mother now lived alone, or if her free-loading siblings were shacked up there, too.

Brett knew she'd cause suspicion if she continued sitting there, watching. So she took a deep breath and drove off to a bar down the road.

There were only a handful of patrons in the place since it was still quite early. Brett was almost surprised to not see any local high school students there. She was pretty sure joints like this didn't enforce the drinking age laws at all.

She heard some whooping, hollering and laughing from a far corner. "Yo! Dude! Check this score!"

"Miller Lite," she said, walking up to the bar.

The bartender didn't bother asking if she wanted a bottle or glass. He plopped a bottle down in front of her. "Two fifty," he said.

She dropped three on the bar and went to investigate the commotion, which she could already tell was focused around a pinball machine. And sure enough, down past the sleepy-looking folks sitting at the bar Brett found the obligatory cigarette machine, a video game and a pinball machine.

Two boys sipping beer were racking the machine for all it was worth. Brett had known there had to be some underagers at the joint. Brett stared for a moment, trying to remember if this place had been here when she'd been growing up, even while she reckoned these boys were probably juniors or seniors in high school. They seemed rather tall for their age, with tidy black hair that poofed up a bit in front, just like Kurt's did. Except his was blond, not black.

"Whatcha lookin' at?" one of them said, noticing her.

"Dyke," the other finished for him.

"Couple of real jerk-off assholes, near as I can tell," Brett said.

"What'd you say, bitch?" the first boy said, turning to face her now as well.

She shrugged. "What can I say? I call 'em like I see 'em." She realized the boys were identical twins. Both wore old, ripped clothes, and for a moment she wondered if the clothes were so awful because the kids came from poor families, or if it was by design, but then she looked at their eyes and realized these two delinquents were related to her. They were her nephews.

She was so taken with this discovery, she almost didn't notice them simultaneously step closer.

But fortunately, she did notice, just in the nick of, as it were.

The nearer one swung a fist at her, which she neatly caught in one hand. She pulled it down, twisting it to force him to turn around, where she locked his arm briefly behind him at an unnatural angle before tossing him at his brother so they both toppled to the floor.

Before they could get off each other, Brett put a foot on the back of the upper one, then leaned onto them, pinning both to the floor momentarily with her weight and strength. Before they could get their acts together and toss her to the side, she pulled her gun out and put it directly against the back of the one on top.

"This is a Smith and Wesson three-fifty-seven with a six-inch barrel. I can kill a fucking elk with it. A lion, even. It will blow through both your worthless asses if I pull this trigger. Now ask yourselves if you want to continue giving me fucking trouble."

"Uh, no," one of them said.

"No what?"

"No, we won't give you no more trouble."

"So you're gonna behave now?"

"Uh, yes."

"Good," Brett said, removing her foot and allowing her gun

to hang by her side. Even she was surprised at how easy it was. God, the years had been a friend to her.

The two boys got up and glowered at her. She made a show of putting her gun away, taking a long pull at her beer, and then turning around. She kept an eye on the boys, however, by their reflections in the dirty window, so when the one behind her to the left grabbed a pool cue and brought it up to strike her, Brett raised her left hand to catch the cue as it whistled toward her. She neatly turned and smashed her fist into his stomach, dropping the bottle just before she did so.

She brought her elbow down and back to strike the other boy in the stomach, while the first doubled over. She kneed the first in the chin so he fell onto his back. Then she grabbed the second by the front of his jacket and slammed him up against the wall so hard the wind was knocked out of him.

This was a little more like it, but still, something felt off.

Brett pulled out her gun again and put it to his head. "You two ain't just ugly and useless, you're stupid motherfuckers as well. I should kill you both here and now and save the world from your stinking existence." She whipped around and kicked the other guy across the room, to the sound of quick applause from the bar. She threw the boy she was holding on top of the first one and then she kicked them both until they were wrapped into themselves and crying.

When she was done, the bartender handed her another beer before quickly putting a few bills into his pocket. "I been waiting a while for somebody to teach those boys some manners."

"It felt damned good," Brett said, downing half the beer. "Do you know their names?"

The barman stared at her for a moment, then looked back at where the boys were slowly bringing themselves to their feet, and back at her. "Jack and Bobby's what I always hear 'em calling each other."

She winked at him, finished her beer and went out to her

SUV, looking around again to see if someone *was* following her.

She couldn't figure out who'd be following her, but still, she didn't leave until she was sure she was alone.

At the old house she parked in front, got out, went to the front door and knocked. And knocked again. Rapped on the window. Rang the bell. And knocked. Until finally a frail-looking old woman answered.

"Yes?" the woman asked, her expression blank.

"Mrs. Higgins?" Brett asked, not quite certain this utterly broken woman was her mother. It had been so many years since she'd seen her. But deep down, she knew this shrunken shell of a woman was her.

"Yes?" the woman said. Brett could see the scars from the various "accidents" her mother had suffered throughout the years.

"Yo! Mom!" a tall, hefty, hairy man said, coming from the back of the house. "Didja find out who was making all the racket?"

"Yes," her mother said, opening the door so he could see Brett while she cowered a bit from the man.

"Whaddya want?" he said to Brett, barely giving her a glance. "Didja get more beer like I told you to?" he asked his mother.

"Ye . . . yes," she stuttered. "I . . . it's in the fridge."

"Good," he said, going to get one. "I'd hate to have to get on you for forgetting again."

Brett looked down at her mother, disgusted that she let Paul walk all over her like that. She couldn't believe she'd wondered why the woman never protected her—she couldn't protect herself. In fact, she'd probably given up years before Brett was born. Hell, the woman didn't even recognize her.

This was all so bloody stupid. Brett strode past her mother and went into the kitchen.

"Who the fuck are you, bitch?" Paul said, taking a pull off his canned beer. Milwaukee's Best. Like father, like son.

Brett froze.

"I asked you a question."

"I asked you a question," Paul said. "You know what happens if I got to ask twice."

"I . . . I don't know," Brett said, huddling in the corner.

First he kicked her. Repeatedly. Then it got bad.

"Don't make me ask twice," he said now, then he backhanded her. She fell to the floor, unable to fight back. "Looks like we got us a fucking intruder on our hands. Why don't you go get me my gun." He wasn't asking their mother a question.

Brett thought about the time some customers broke into Storm's house, after repeatedly harassing her. Brett had killed one of them during the fight. And now she was thinking that her brother was about to kill her in cold blood without a fight because she couldn't move.

Then her mother looked up at Paul. "I . . . I can't. Let's call the police or—"

Paul backhanded her so hard she hit the wall.

Brett realized there were a woman and two children standing, frightened, in the front door.

She thought about her philandering, bullying and abusive father, and how he'd passed along all of his worst traits to his offspring. She thought about her own ways—how she had killed and beaten folks and how she'd cheated on Allie. Maybe she was like them.

And here was more of her generation, and their mother had tried to stop him—and he'd hit his own mother. Her mother hadn't escaped her abuse when Brett's father had died, because he'd trained his children well.

"Get me my gun," Paul said. Loudly. One of the children scurried to get it.

Brett had never stood up to her family before. She'd even frozen when two of them had confronted her at the theater.

"P-Paul," her mother said, from where she lay on the floor. "Y-you can't. Not her." She tried to stand.

63

Brett had managed to stand up to two of her nephews at a bar. "This piece a shit?" Paul said, turning and kicking Brett.

She took down worse than this guy every day of the week and twice when she was pissed. The little boy stood with a gun, watching as Paul kicked Brett again and again.

Brett gasped for air, curling up like one of those loser boys in that bar.

Brett couldn't believe she was about to meet her end in the house she'd escaped so many years before. She thought about Storm. She thought about Allie. She thought about Victoria. And wished she could live to tell any of them good-bye.

"Stop!" Brett recognized the voice, but was almost past caring. She was sure she had to be hallucinating, because it surely couldn't be who she was sure it sounded like. There was no way it could be. No way at all . . .

She thought she might pass out. She was glad that'd be the last voice she heard before she died, though.

"And what are you gonna do about it?" Paul asked.

"Shoot you. Probably kill you."

"Yeah—"

Brett heard the gun go off. She didn't know who shot whom, or what happened, exactly. She should care, and she thought she might, but she couldn't focus her mind, nor could she see past the pain enough to do so. She really thought she was going to pass out, and she could only focus on not crying before she did so. After all, she didn't want any of her family to ever see her cry again.

"You missed," Brett's brother Paul said.

"I meant to. Next one hits you. But I won't kill you right away, just put you in a lot of pain," Victoria said.

"Give me that," Paul said to the child. There was another shot, and then Paul screamed in pain.

"You," Victoria said to the child with the gun. "Hand that over to me." Apparently, she got it, because even as Paul whined in pain, she went to Brett. "Come on, baby, it's going to be all right."

Brett let Victoria help her stand. She realized she hadn't been being paranoid when she thought someone was following her, she'd been realizing her guardian angel was watching over her, and she should just ignore her, 'cause she'd only step in when she was needed.

Dear God, she was getting stupid and melodramatic in her old, beaten age.

"You shot my husband!" the woman in the door screamed, running to beat on Victoria.

"Goddamnit!" Paul yelled. "Somebody fuckin' call nine-one-one already!"

Brett grabbed the woman who had been beating on Victoria and threw her out of the way, yelling, "Calm down!" before wrapping her arms around Victoria.

"You fuckin' calm down! She shot my husband!"

"You shouldn't be here. You don't have to be doing this," Victoria told Brett.

"You two are going to prison and never getting out!" the wife screamed at them, as Brett casually pinned her against the wall.

"Not in the least," Victoria told her. "He was attacking her."

"She broke in!" Paul yelled.

"No," Brett's mother said.

Brett looked at her. "Do you know who I am?"

"Yes."

"Do you know what Laura asked me?"

"Yes."

"Do you want me involved?"

"Yes."

And Paul continued to whimper and whine. "You goddamn bitches are gonna pay for this!"

Brett knelt next to him. She stuck a finger in his gunshot wound. He screamed in pain. She looked at where her mother lay. "Should I stop?"

It was kinda like everything stopped for a moment. Even the wife stayed put. Maybe she hadn't been married to Paul long enough to truly hate him, or else it had all been a show up till then . . .

And Brett's mother said, "No."

Brett looked into Paul's eyes. "Not so fun doing all the getting like this, eh?"

"What the fuck is your problem?" he yelled back.

"If I wind up saving your sorry ass, it'll be for Mom and Laura," Brett said.

"What the hell are you talking about?" he said, tears running down his face from the pain.

"Your sister's back," Victoria said. "And she's one big bad-ass that hates your fucking guts. But she's probably your only chance to not get killed."

"You're little shithead?" Paul said.

"Probably not the right thing to say to a woman who carries a gun that's six times longer than your penis," Victoria said.

"I'll likely kill you if you ever refer to me like that again," Brett said, kicking Paul. "Or touch me like that again." She kicked him again.

Victoria laid a restraining hand on her arm before she laid into him with the kicking. It was as if Victoria knew there was a fine line between abuser and abused, and how quickly the latter could become the former . . . *And of course she does.*

Sirens indicated the cops had arrived. Brett was surprised it hadn't taken much, much longer.

"You should probably leave," Brett told Victoria. She wondered if she could ever thank her enough for following her today, or if she could ever tell her all the stories about herself and Storm.

"No. I'm not leaving you alone in this house again," Victoria said, and with one look into Brett's eyes, she told Brett that she

66

followed only because she knew and understood and that Brett should never, ever, try to explain, because it would hurt them both way too much.

Two police officers arrived at the door, rapping loudly on the frame. "We got a report of a domestic disturbance, and then a nine-one-one call for help with a shooting," the smaller cop said. His uniform was quite neat and tidy.

"Yes!" the wife yelled. "This woman"—she indicated Brett— "broke in, and when my husband tried to subdue her, her friend came in and shot him!"

"S-s-she didn't break in," Martha Higgins, Brett's mother, said. "S-s-she's my daughter. I asked her in."

"Call the paramedics," the cop in charge said to his cohort.

Brett walked out of the room, while the police were focused on the injured. Victoria followed her. The house was even more run-down than Brett remembered. She went upstairs. Many of the rooms no longer even had doors.

In her folks' old room she found everything almost the way it had been, but now her father's clothing and other possessions were gone. And when she glanced through the drawers, she found, hidden under her mother's underwear (very plain, old-lady cotton stuff), a few dozen articles about her. Like her mother had been keeping track of her. Like maybe her mother had been proud of her. Like maybe her survival had cut through her mom's evil existence to mean something—to tell her that sometimes folks could survive.

"Thank you," Brett said to Victoria.

"Don't ever say that again."

"I need to, when you save my life like that."

"You would've worked things out on your own."

"I don't know—"

Victoria grabbed her and kissed her hard, letting her know how much she loved her and how she belonged to Brett.

Brett walked into her old room and checked out the view of

the rotting neighborhood. She fingered the doorway, which had been bashed in much during her time there. The frame was practically splinters now, and the door nonexistent.

Victoria wrapped herself around Brett from behind.

"Why's his wife and kids standing by him?" Brett asked.

"Because they're afraid."

"Who all do you reckon live here now?"

"I dunno. Your fuckhead brother and his wife," Victoria said. "Maybe their kids—those two little 'uns, in the other. Your mother in another." She walked back around, looking around the last two rooms. "Brother and his wife in one. Kids, likely boys, in the last."

"What are you doing up here?" the first cop asked.

"Checking out my old room," Brett said.

"You two have been accused of breaking and entering, plus assault and battery, shooting and more. And now you're simply sightseeing through the house?"

"I didn't break," Brett said. "And I was the one attacked when I was *invited* in. Mention that to my psychotic, abusive bro, and tell him if he presses charges—against either of us—so will I."

"I'll see what I can do," the cop said. "But you need to give a statement as well, Ms. Higgins."

"Yo, don't call me that . . . and so you believe me?"

"I already know who you are. And I've been called here before. I'm glad to see one of these get what they deserve. But I didn't say that."

When Brett came back downstairs, her mother grabbed her hand and said, "I'm sorry we didn't let you know about your father's death."

"I'm not," Brett replied. She walked over to one of the children. "Hi, I'm Brett."

The child ran across the room to his mother.

And pretty much that was how the opening of her investigation went. No one wanted to talk with her. They fled without saying a word. She worried that'd be indicative of the rest of it as well.

Then Laura arrived, immediately putting an arm around Martha, who was being seen to by the paramedics. "Oh, Mother, are you all right?"

Brett glared at Laura, wondering what brought her here, especially now.

"Thank you for bringing her back to me," Martha said, burying her face in Laura's neck.

"I don't know what your problem is," the wife finally said to Brett. "But you should leave and never come back."

"Marie will be so happy," Martha said toward Brett while Laura went to check on the rest of the family.

"What?" Brett said.

"She'll be happy you finally came back to me. I know how you loved each other."

"Hold on," Brett said. "Have you seen Marie?"

"Oh, yes," Martha said. "I remember Marie. Merry. Didn't you call her that?"

"Where and when did you see her?" Brett asked.

"I . . . I don't remember. But it wasn't that long ago . . ."

Brett refused to let her hopes get up. Her mother seemed to have given up any bit of reality long ago, too long ago for Brett to lay any faith in what she said, let alone count on her words to let her even think she might ever see Merry again. Brett thought about asking Laura, but Laura would tell her whatever she had to to get her involved in the investigation—even lie about Merry being around. Of that Brett was sure.

"Okay," the cop said. "Do I got this right? Nobody's pressing charges against anybody?"

"No!" the wife screamed. "We're pressing charges against this lunatic!"

"Listen," Brett said. "You press charges against me, and I'll press charges against Paul—and guess who's gonna win?"—and before the woman could say one word—"the one with the most cha-ching for a truly great lawyer. Plus, being utterly, totally and completely justified will help our side of the matter."

"Chriss," Laura said, coming up behind the wife, "you should listen to this woman. You won't end up on top."

"Man," one of the boys whose ass Brett had just well and thoroughly kicked, said, coming in the front door, "you shoulda . . ." He paused, as if assessing who all was in the room.

"Seen all the guys that jumped us!" his brother filled in.

"Oh really?" Brett said, her arms crossed in front of her as she looked down at them.

"You!"

"Jackie, Bobby," Laura said, "I'd like you to meet your Aunt Brett. Brett, these young men are Jackie and Bobby, your nephews."

"The one who beat your asses," Brett said, grabbing Laura by the elbow and pulling her outside. "What the fuck are you doing here?"

"I knew you'd be stopping by," Laura said. "I'd already told Martha about it, but I wanted to let the others know."

"So you stopping here now is just coincidence?" Brett said.

"Well, yes."

"I'm keeping an eye on you, 'cause I really ain't buying that you're innocent and it's all just coincidence," Brett said, going out to her car with Victoria. She made sure Victoria was safe and driving away before she herself left.

Chapter Eight

Brett hadn't planned on being around when Allie stopped by that night. She knew she could trust her, and didn't need all the issues being around her would bring up yet again. But that night, when Allie showed up with Rowan, Brett was sitting on the sofa watching *Planet Terror*, laughing and drinking a beer.

Allie looked over at her. Then she stopped, staring at Brett's obvious injuries. "My God, Brett—what happened?" She ran to kneel by Brett.

"I went to visit my mother today."

"Your mother did this?" Allie asked.

"No. My brother did. And when he got a gun and was about to shoot me, kill me," Brett said, "it wasn't you there to stop him."

"What happened?" Allie asked.

"No, you can't ask that. You told me to get into this—you

threw me into it, and you weren't there for me. We've been lovers for how many years? And yet you didn't know . . ."

"What can I know when you don't let me in?"

"Well, here's a clue: Ask."

"God," Rowan said. "Did you take extra bitch pills today or what?"

"I'm going out now," Brett said, tossing on her black leather trench coat. "I just wanted to make sure you saw what doing what you told me to do did to me." She had to have an exit line. She could not possibly have this conversation with Allie now—especially not in front of Rowan.

"You could've fought back," Rowan said.

"You weren't there. You don't know what happened," Brett said. "You don't know how there wasn't a goddamn way in the world that I could've fought back."

After Brett left, Allie stared after her.

"C'mon," Rowan said. "Let's get what we came for."

"I'm worried about her."

"She's a big girl, I'm sure she can take care of herself."

"You have no idea what she's going through."

"From what you've said, neither do you," Rowan said, leading them toward the basement door. "You said your stuff is in the basement, right?"

"I know she didn't have a good time with her family. She hasn't seen any of them since she left home for college."

"And what does that have to do with the price of rice in China?"

"From everything I've seen and heard, they were extraordinarily abusive. Brett was lucky to have made it out alive."

"And so that makes everything she did to you—everything she put you through—all right?"

"No, but it makes me feel responsible for what's happening to her right now. I put her up to it, and I'm sure she's doing it because of me."

"From what I've seen and heard, she's not willing to deal with her issues, and not willing to be a hundred percent responsible for her actions. There's nothing you can do about that, Allie." Rowan turned to look at her. She ran a hand along Allie's cheek. "The best thing you can do is to save yourself."

"But I love her, Rowan."

"And what has she done to earn that love, Allie?"

"Well, she took a bullet for me and—"

"What has she done *lately*—besides sleep with other women?"

Allie stared at Rowan for a moment, then turned toward the downstairs door. "The stuff's in the basement. Let's get it and go."

Brett went back inside to get a soda from the fridge and take a peek downstairs, just in time to catch Allie and Rowan embracing. The why didn't really matter to her, she just couldn't believe they were doing it in her own basement.

Brett didn't know where to go, so she went to her second home: The Paradise Theater. If she didn't know where Allie was, she'd likely have driven by Rowan's on her way to the theater. She couldn't believe Allie'd suggested mutual nonmonogamy, but this she could believe even less. Allie knew how wrecked she was, and still she was practically getting it on with Rowan in Brett's own basement. It was wholly and totally unbelievable and there was no excuse for it, no reason for it.

Brett parked in the lot, nodded to the security guard, who, she gleefully noted, was actually awake, sober and paying attention to what was happening. She went into the theater, nodded to the clerk, who was also amazingly alert, and used her key to go through the door. She glanced at her watch and, seeing the time, went right into the auditorium.

She sat in the middle of the theater and watched as Exposé finished her set, then headed into the audience to do lap dances. Expo apparently didn't realize at first who she was, but as she approached to ask if Brett wanted a lap dance, she stopped.

"Oh, you," Expo said. "I expect you're waiting for Victoria, huh?"

"Yeah, baby. I'm sorry." She'd always liked Expo, who was very professional about her job.

"So should I let her know . . . or not?"

"How 'bout not?" Little did Expo know that she'd ensured a few extra bookings with this point of consideration.

"You got it, boss," Expo said with a wink before she exited the theater.

Nicky, the clerk, introduced Victoria. "And now here's the hot, hot Tempest!" The clerks weren't too creative with their intros.

The first time Brett had heard Victoria's new music, she'd had to ask Victoria about the songs she'd chosen. This first number was "Stupid Thing" by Nickel. It was a slow, driving beat that, when Victoria moved to it, was totally seductive.

Victoria strode down the aisle and up to the stage, her figure almost entirely covered by her long, black trench coat. She turned her back to the audience, moving her hips to the music, and slowly dropped the coat to the floor. She grooved to the music, with her back still to the audience, wearing a black leather vest, skintight low riders and high black boots.

She turned toward the audience and Brett immediately got hot seeing that Victoria already had the button undone on her jeans. And now, as she moved and swayed, lost in her own little world, she pulled down the zipper on her jeans, unbuttoned her vest, unzipped her boots, and pulled them off.

The music segued into Madonna's "Hung Up." Victoria transitioned into the faster pace as it sped up, tossing off more clothing as she went, till she was down to her lacy red bra, panties, thigh-high stockings and stilettos.

Then the music went into total manic with 2 Unlimited's "Twilight Zone," the rave remix. And it was when Victoria was thrusting and getting naked and driving the boys wild that Victoria apparently realized Brett was in the audience. Their gazes met for a moment, as Victoria opened herself up, and Brett was sure the rest of the act was subtly changed from then on.

Brett kept a close watch while Tempest gave the other patrons lap dances. She tried to distract herself by watching the images that flickered across the screen, but het porn wasn't her thing. Pretty much, she was so over porn it had no effect on her anymore. Years of exposure to it could do such things, she figured.

Most of all, she tried not to think about Luke and Laura, and about her family and her past and—

"Lap dance?" Victoria said, walking up to her.

Oh yes, she'd also been trying not to watch Victoria being almost naked with all the male patrons of the theater.

Brett pulled her wallet out of the breast pocket of her trench coat. She pulled out a hundred-dollar bill. Victoria straddled her on her chair. Brett put the bill in the waist of her G-string.

Victoria pulled the bill out and shoved it into Brett's pocket. "Never try to pay me for anything I do for you." She began to move on Brett's lap. She wore her G-string and bra.

Until, of course, she removed her bra. The dancers were supposed to keep on a top and a bottom while performing lap dances, though Brett knew most of her dancers broke that rule. But she was pretty sure Victoria never did. Until now, that was.

"Did my sister ever dance for you like this?" Victoria asked, her breasts rubbing against Brett's face.

Brett shoved her back. "Stop comparing yourself to your sister. I loved her, I love you, but you're different people."

Victoria stared at her for a moment, then moved down to kiss her hard and deep. Brett was taken aback for a moment, then she pulled Victoria into her, sliding her tongue along Victoria's, holding her warm, bare skin close . . .

"I want you," Brett whispered into her ear.

"I have another show tonight."

"I'm the boss. Skip it. Let's go to your place. Now."

"No."

"Are you saying no to me?"

"Yes. I have a job."

"And I'm your boss."

"I don't mix business with pleasure."

"You won't even let me give you the rest of the night off for saving my life today?"

"No. But we can go upstairs to your office till the next show," Victoria said, pulling her bra back on and . . .

Brett reached up to close the clasp on Victoria's bra. "God, I'm not good at this. I'm actually not sure I've ever *fastened* another woman's bra before."

"You're really hurting," Victoria said, holding Brett's head in her hands and looking into her eyes. She apparently could see something in Brett that Brett was hiding from herself. "Wait at the door for me." She went and collected her costume, then led Brett through the box office upstairs to her office, where again she held Brett while Brett cried.

But this time, as Victoria stroked Brett's back and Brett's tears began to subside, no one interrupted them. Plus, Victoria wore almost no clothing.

Brett's head was in Victoria's lap, and she began to nuzzle Victoria's thighs as her hands caressed Victoria's body—knees to ankles, from her waist up her back. She began to kiss up Victoria's tummy . . .

"Brett, what's going on?" Victoria asked, pulling Brett's face to look up at her.

Instead of answering, Brett pulled down the straps of

Victoria's bra, revealing her breasts. She tongued and kissed her way down Victoria's neck, toward her breasts.

"He beat on you pretty hard today, aren't you hurting? You should have gone to the hospital."

"I've learned to ignore the pain." Brett licked and kissed Victoria's breasts, closing in on her nipples.

Victoria grabbed a handful of Brett's hair and pulled her head away from her. "I don't want to be with you when I know you're thinking about her."

"I'm not thinking about her. I'm not thinking about them," Brett said, lifting herself up to look directly into Victoria's eyes. "And when we were together before, I was only thinking about you."

"Brett . . ."

"What?"

"You know . . ." It was as if Victoria couldn't finish the sentence of her own free will.

Brett sat up to hold Victoria, gently and as nonsexually as she could possibly hold an almost naked woman. She reached over to grab the blanket that lay along the back of her couch and pull it around Victoria, to cover her.

"You're the only person I've ever been with of my choosing," Victoria finally said.

Brett took a deep breath while still holding Victoria and running her fingers lightly over Victoria's body in what she hoped was a reassuring manner. "I'm not a good person to choose."

"You're wrong," Victoria said, pulling up slightly. "You are a good person, Brett Higgins. You've done a lot of good in your life. You've just painted yourself as a bad person, and allowed others to do the same as well."

"So where do I go from here?"

"You figure out who's doing in your family, then you decide what to do about it. What happens with Allie will happen—you'll continue doing whatever you're doing about that."

"And you're okay with that?"

"Brett, I love you. I love you so much I can't stand in the way of what you think you must do, who you have to have . . . be with."

Brett watched Victoria throughout the next show, and then followed her home after.

It turned out that Victoria also knew where Allie was staying, because she drove by there en route—even parking across the street and walking back to say to Brett, "I'll wait in my car while you scope things out."

Brett reached out to grab Victoria's wrist. "No need." Brett kissed her wrist. "Take me to yours."

They were sixteen and at a barbecue at a relative's a bit of a drive away. Brett remembered that day for what happened—with Merry, and how her dad got arrested for drunken driving while the entire family was in the car.

Her mother was also drunk, as was everyone in the car who had a driver's license. All that night, Brett hoped she'd be taken from her family, even as she worried about that happening, because that might mean she might never see Merry again.

Earlier in the day, when Merry had first seen her, Merry grabbed her arm and pulled her away from all the others. It was what they always tried to do. Not only did they want to not attract any unwanted attention from the rest of the family, but also they wanted the time they could get for themselves.

"Brett," she said, pulling them into a shed. "I . . ."

"What?"

Merry gulped and looked down. "I can't take any more of this. I'm not as strong as you are."

"Merry, you are *strong. You* can *make it through." They'd never shared precise details about anything, but Brett was pretty sure she knew what Merry was going through. After all, their fathers were brothers.*

"Brett, I don't know . . . I just want you to know . . ." She held Brett's head, hard. She pulled at Brett's hair. She pushed herself up

against Brett. "Brett," she whispered into Brett's ear, "I need you to touch me. Kiss me. Please."

"What's going on, Merry?" Brett said, pulling back slightly.

"When everything gets dark, remembering you is the only way I get through. Please. I need for something in this life to happen by my own choice." She took Brett's hand in her own and placed it on her breast. "Please."

Looking back, all these years later, Brett realized Marie was probably already on the junk. She was either strung out or jonesing for another hit when it happened, but still, Brett wanted to know more.

And now she followed Victoria to Victoria's little one-bedroom apartment at the southern edge of Warren, right along the demarcation line between Warren and Detroit. It wasn't a great location, not the safest in the world—but much safer than Storm's place had been.

"Give me this, please," Merry had pleaded that day. "Give me something good and right in my life. We've been heading here since we were babies, practically."

Brett followed Victoria up the stairs and into the apartment. Victoria went to her fridge, grabbed a Miller Lite for herself and one for Brett. She handed the beer to Brett, then turned on the radio.

Brett sat on the couch and, when Victoria made to sit next to her, pulled her into her lap. "I need to be close to you."

Victoria relaxed into Brett, leaning against her.

Brett couldn't resist Merry. She'd started wanting to kiss her long before they kissed. And then she wanted to get even closer, but was afraid she'd scare Merry off with that.

And now Merry was asking for it. She'd put Brett's hand on her breast and everything! There was no misinterpreting this! But appar-ently Merry saw the fear in Brett's eyes and the hesitation in her touch. No matter what, Brett couldn't believe that all this good could come into her lap at once. She couldn't believe dreams could come true. Merry pulled off her T-shirt. Then she kicked off her shoes. "Lift me onto the bench," she said.

Brett picked her up by her hips and lifted her onto the workbench she had been standing in front of.

"Brett, I need you to touch me."

Brett knew exactly what Merry meant with that statement, but she couldn't believe it.

"Victoria," Brett now said, holding her on her lap.

"Yes?"

"What's going on?"

"You're holding me." Victoria turned on her lap to look at her. "Brett, you wouldn't believe how much I love you."

"I love you, too."

"No, I mean . . . I mean that . . . I mean that sitting here on my couch, with you holding me, is a fantasy come true."

Brett couldn't believe she could ever mean so much to anyone. But now Merry was sitting here saying it.

"W-w-what do you mean?" Brett asked.

Merry put her head on Brett's shoulder. "Don't make me explain. Just . . . Make me yours. In all ways. At least for now."

Brett couldn't believe every one of her dreams was coming true right now. But she was tired of always being afraid. So now, she decided she had to at least try to get what she wanted. She ran her fingers, her hands, up and down Merry's back, enjoying the silken feel of her skin, trying to ignore the scars, until she finally undid Merry's bra and pulled it off her.

Merry had taken off her shirt herself, so Brett reckoned she had reason to think Merry wanted her to take her bra off. And if she didn't, if Brett was doing something wrong, Brett hoped Merry would let her know.

She didn't want to do anything to Merry that Merry didn't want, after all.

Brett kissed Merry's jaw, and neck, and cupped her breasts.

Merry wrapped her legs and arms around Brett, pulling her closer.

"Brett, I love you. Being with you might have been the single most important moment in my life. When I met you, I think I maybe wanted to kill you, but . . . God, Brett," Victoria said.

"Baby," Brett said, burying her face in Victoria's shoulder, "I'm a mess. You shouldn't love me."

"Do not fucking tell me you're not lovable—or not *worthy* of love."

"I fuck up everything I touch!"

"You do not! Look at your business! Look at you compared to your family!"

"Fine. I can make money. No big. But I can't commit. I can't be with someone. I can't love."

Brett cupped Merry's breasts, exploring them gradually, enjoying the feel of Merry's nipples against the palms of her hands.

"Brett—oh, God, Brett . . ."

Brett thumbed her nipples.

"Baby, do I need to draw you a diagram?"

Brett looked up at Merry. "What do you mean?" She looked back down at Marie's naked breasts, at her hard and erect nipples.

Merry leaned back, and pulled down the zipper on her jeans. "I want—I need—to be naked for you. I need to feel you inside me."

"Brett, I constantly think about how I want to end it all. And all the reasons I shouldn't even try to go on. I think about all sorts of bad things, and the biggest thing that keeps me going is you."

"That's not right."

"The second biggest reason is to be able to stand up to my family like you can with yours. You can show all those losers how successful and powerful and important you are now. I want to be able to do that sometime, too."

"Victoria. I love you. But I also love Allie. And I loved your sister, too."

Victoria stood and brought Brett with her. She pushed off Brett's coat and draped it across the couch. She took Brett's hands in her own and led her to the bedroom, where she lit the candle next to the bed.

Brett had been staring at her ass as she bent to light the candle. When she turned back to Brett, Brett stared, then said, "Damn, you're hot. And you've got a great ass."

Victoria pulled off her own T-shirt, then pulled off Brett's black V-necked shirt and burgundy V-necked sweater.

Victoria sat on the bed and pulled off her own boots and socks. Then she leaned back and said, "Take off my jeans."

Brett stood, staring at her.

Merry leaned forward to put Brett's hands on her waistband. "Please."

Brett fell to her knees. "This isn't right."

Merry leaned forward to whisper in her ear, "Nothing that's happened to us has been right."

Brett looked up and suddenly realized that Merry'd been strong enough for long enough. Everything Brett now said would take even more from Merry, who'd already had more than enough.

Brett got down on her knees and pulled off Victoria's jeans.

Brett pulled off Merry's jeans and panties. And then she stood up. And looked down at Merry, who was now naked. Merry tried, momentarily, to cover herself, but Brett stopped that.

Brett gazed down at all of Merry's charms, until Merry relaxed her

thighs and arms and let Brett gaze at her fully exposed form.
"Brett, please," Merry said. "Tell me if—"
Brett dropped to her knees and stared at Merry's cunt. She ran her
hands up and down Merry's thighs, even as she licked lightly up her
inner thighs.

Victoria helped Brett to her feet, then stripped Brett of the rest of her clothing. By the time Brett realized what was happening, they were both naked.

"I need to feel you against me," Victoria said, pulling Brett down on top of her.

Brett was used to being in control, to being in charge. And even though she was now on top, still, she didn't feel as in control as she used to—due to the entire lack of clothing and everything.

But it felt so good to have her bare nipples against Victoria's bare skin.

Almost as good as it felt to have all her naked skin against all of Victoria's naked skin.

Brett put her thigh between Victoria's thighs, then she slipped her finger in . . .

Merry held Brett back. "Don't do anything you don't want to."
Brett looked up at Merry. Then she closed her eyes and dropped her
forehead against Merry's right thigh. "I've dreamt of this . . . fanta-
sized about it . . . I knew I could never be close enough to you . . . I
always thought it was wrong and I was sick and—"
"You're not the sick one," Merry said, pulling Brett up into her
arms. Merry leaned back onto the counter, her legs still spread for
Brett.
"Merry, please, you're the only person I trust. Tell me this isn't a
trick."
"It isn't a trick, Brett."
Brett was back down on her knees, between Merry's legs. She lifted

her mouth up to suckle at one of Merry's tits. She ran her hands up
Merry's thighs.
And then down them.
And then Merry took her right hand into her own hand.

Victoria held Brett tightly against her as Brett fingered her.
She left the candle burning and looked right into Brett's eyes as
she approached orgasm.
Brett leaned down to kiss her, and they still kept their eyes
open, looking into one another.

Merry guided Brett's hand up her thigh, and then helped Brett slip
her fingers inside her.
"Oh, yes, Brett," Merry said.
Brett knelt at Merry's feet and looked up at her. Bringing her fin-
gers outside to caress her clit, then sliding them back into her. "Can I
touch you . . . anywhere?"
Merry looked down at her. "Yes."

Victoria grabbed her ass, pulling her in close. Victoria raised her
thigh, to rub between Brett's legs. And even as Brett spread her legs,
pushing herself against Victoria, and reaching between Victoria's
legs to finger her, and dip her finger into Victoria's wet and spread it
around, Victoria reached up to yank on Brett's nipples.
"Bad girl," Brett said, bringing her arms up to push Victoria's
hands from her breasts. But Victoria grasped her hard enough
that it took a bit for her to release her hold on Brett's nipples.
"You've got great tits," Victoria said. "I'll let you finger and
fuck me as long as you let me suck and tease them."
When Brett dropped down, to keep her breasts from
Victoria, Victoria closed her legs and pulled away from her.

Merry spread herself out, watching as Brett's fingers went into and
out of her body, and as Brett licked and nibbled at her breasts.

Brett had three fingers inside Merry and was pulling Merry's right nipple with her teeth, when she looked up at Merry.

Merry looked down at her. "Don't fuck me," she said.

Brett pulled away. Suddenly. Jerkily.

Merry grabbed her hand, stilling it inside herself. "No, I like you inside me. I like you touching me. I like you . . . fucking me."

"So what do you mean?"

Merry waited a few moments. "Take off your clothes."

"What?"

"I want to feel you against me."

"Do you think it's bad or wrong if it feels good to you, Brett?" Victoria said. She reached over to her bedside table to pull out a strap-on. She handed it to Brett and pulled out lube. "Put this on. I bought it for you."

Brett pulled it on, tightening it. Then she let Victoria lube her up and ride her.

But when she was all the way inside Victoria, Victoria leaned down to rub their nipples together and to kiss Brett. As she rode Brett, she played with herself, running her hands up and down her body, further enticing and turning Brett on.

Victoria reached down to grab Brett's nipples.

Brett pulled off her clothes. Well, down to her underwear. And after Brett had slowly fit her fist into Merry, Merry grabbed Brett's nipples. And it felt so fucking damned good to have her yanking and pulling on them so tight and hard . . .

And then Merry shoved her hand into Brett's shorts and ran her fingers up and down Brett's wet, feeling her up and fingering her.

"Get naked," Merry said.

And Brett complied.

Victoria had Brett's dick all the way inside, and she rode it at a pace, even as she pulled and squeezed at Brett's nipples.

Victoria brought Brett's hands up over her head. "Hold on until I tell you to let go. Don't listen, and I might leave." She made Brett hold on to the headboard.

And she continued to touch herself and Brett, and play with both of them as well.

But now, with Brett's arms held above her head, she felt she could play a bit more. Now she pulled out the nipple clamps and was surprised that Brett didn't argue against them from the get-go; instead, Brett kept asking her to crank them up tighter.

Brett both hated and loved her position.

Chapter Nine

November 11

Brett awoke the next morning curled around Allie. She buried her face in the luxuriant hair and breathed deeply.

It wasn't Allie.

Victoria turned around in her arms. "Hey, lover," she said.

"Hey, gorgeous," Brett said, leaning forward to kiss her neck.

"Oh, God," Victoria replied, stretching and pushing against Brett. "I love waking up with you."

"Hmm, you do, do you?"

"But unfortunately, today I have to work—and I have to be there in forty-five minutes." The first show was at ten a.m. Usually Brett liked for the girls to be there at least fifteen minutes early, but she wouldn't charge them extra unless they actually were late, or a known troublemaker. "Yeah, and you know what a hardass my boss can be."

"God yes. What a bitch! Tell you what—you take a shower

and I'll cook us up something to eat."

"Mmm, sounds wonderful. But I'm almost tempted to ask you to join me for a shower, instead."

Brett knew a lot of folks considered a shared shower the utmost in intimacy. She didn't follow that belief. "Sounds great—but I don't want you cursing me in a few hours because you didn't eat."

"We could be quick and do both," Victoria said.

Brett slapped Victoria's ass. "Get going. I'll rummage through the kitchen."

After breakfast, Brett went back to her place and called into the theater, to let the clerk know she was the reason Tempest might've been a bit late and to let Frankie know she was working on the case, so probably wouldn't be in. She knew she could simply tell Frankie she was responsible for Victoria's tardiness, but she didn't think Frankie would like that they'd spent the night together.

She went into the study and pulled up her listing of family to investigate. She added lines about the two nephews she'd met the day before, as well as annotating Paul's listing and adding lines for Paul's wife and children as well.

To stop by, interview and check in on all of the relatives she'd unearthed so far would take quite a while. Fortunately, she came from a long line of white trash, so sometimes multiple families lived under one roof, which would greatly simplify things for her.

Nonetheless, she hated that they so obviously took to heart the lines about "go forth and multiply" in her family. Yup, they were good Christian stock, following only the bits of the Bible that they picked and chose, just like Fundamentalist types. Granted, Fundamentalist types weren't usually so obvious about their breaking of the laws and preferred, instead, to hide any indiscretions behind whatever closed doors they could.

• • •

Brett had six brothers: Matthew, Mark, Luke, John, Peter and Paul, all of whom were older than her. Her father, Matthew and John were dead, so she'd spiral out with Mark, Luke, Peter and Paul. To begin with. Them and their spouses and families, that was.

She'd already met Paul and his wife, Chriss, and their two kids. The entire family lived with her mother. But she didn't want to try to get anything out of Chriss at this point, so she'd move on down the list, which was rather easy, since Mark and Peter lived together.

She drove over to sit across the street from their house in Warren. Most folks didn't know that Warren was the third largest city in the state. Most folks had never even heard of it. Like so many areas of Michigan, it was terribly segregated—for instance, barely any black people lived north of Eleven Mile.

Her brothers lived in a house at about Eight-and-a-half—south of Nine Mile—right around Ryan. It was a cookie-cutter neighborhood, with not much differentiating one home from another, except perhaps the thin lines dividing up-and-coming from white trash and white trashiest.

Her brother's lawn was unkempt, as was nearly everything about their home. But it didn't stand apart in any way from the other houses on the street.

She got out of her car to knock on their front door.

When there was no answer, she rang the bell.

Then she waited some more. And finally glanced through the front windows and circled round back, seeing if there were any indications anyone was home.

"Who the fuck are you, and what the fuck are you doing?"

Brett turned around. She knew that tone of voice, and would usually respond by diving and pulling out her own gun, but it was daytime in a suburb, so she didn't think there was a real threat going on.

She was wrong.

Mark was facing her, holding a shotgun aimed right at her chest.

She automatically froze at the sight of him. Wearing a dirty wife-beater tank and blue pants, he was older and fatter, but she could still recognize him. She took a breath and put her hands out away from herself. "Yo, dude, I'm here to help you."

"I don't need no help with nothing."

"Your father and two of your brothers have been killed recently, as well as some other relatives. I'd say you definitely have something to worry about."

"Is that a threat?"

"No. I already said, I'm here to help you."

"My little baby's here to do that," Mark said, patting his shotgun.

"Even when you're dead drunk asleep?"

"So who are you that you give a shit about me and mine?" He lowered the gun almost imperceptibly, while his little beady eyes got even beadier, showing that he was paying attention to her.

She didn't like him, didn't trust him, and she knew she had to do something about it. The problem was unfreezing her joints and forcing herself to move—before he did anything to her. Victoria had saved her yesterday. Today it was up to her. She stepped to the side while grabbing the barrel of the gun, pushing it down and away before latching onto it with her other hand and yanking it from Mark's grasp.

Her heart was pounding in her chest all the while. When she spoke, she had to hide her breathlessness. "I'm someone your sister-in-law came to asking for help for the family." She flipped the gun around so she held it with the barrel pointing toward the ground.

"Which one?"

"Laura."

"And why'd she come to you?"

"Because she heard about me. She heard Luke talk about me. And she read in the papers that I solved problems. That I had money and power and could fix things."

"So if you're so big and important, why the fuck don't I recognize you?"

"Because you might as well have blown your brains out years ago with all the booze and drugs you've done." She wanted to kick him in the nuts or slam the shotgun into his balls, but she knew she'd likely have to deal with him again soon—and he wouldn't be nearly as antagonistic toward her if she didn't neuter him beforehand.

"That's little sister," Peter said, coming around from the front of the house. He was nowhere near as large as most of the family. He was of average height, slender build, and seemed like some sort of a wormy accountant in his off-the-rack polyester suit. He stopped next to Mark. "Brett, I think they called her."

"So this is little Brett, huh?" Mark said. "Maybe we should get all reacquainted with lil' sis." He stepped toward her, his hand going automatically to his zipper.

Peter threw out his arm. "No. I think maybe we should listen to what she has to say. For now, at least." He was quite the snively sort. All Brett could think about when looking at him was a weasel.

And that was what pushed Brett through the old memories, what pushed her back into today, and who she was now. She was in charge now, damnit. She shoved aside the barrel of the gun, pulled out her .357 and put it to Mark's chin. "I'm here to help— not to put up with your bullshit."

"Oh, Brett," Peter said, his hands crossed in front of his crotch. "If you were serious, you would have done that before I stepped in." He stood still, watching her through his Coke-bottle glasses, looking for all the world like a tax accountant. "So our darling sister-in-law contacted you because somebody is apparently killing all your relations." He moved toward her, then looked her up and down. "What I don't understand is why you care? From what I've read, I wouldn't imagine you to be the sort to care much about . . . blood relations, shall we say? Especially not us. Not unless you totally forgot how much fun we all used to have, that is."

At this distance, Brett could see how greasy his slicked-back hair was. She could also see his nose and ear hairs. And, since she was happily taller than he, she could also tell that his hair was thinning across the top. "Someone overheard Laura asking me for help, and asked me to look into it."

"Must be somebody rather important for you to actually talk to us. I imagine she has quite a lot of influence over you, hmm?"

"*Her?*" Mark said, stepping forward with his hand going to his zipper yet again. "*She?* Maybe I oughta pay her a visit, huh? Give her more of that special Higgins treatment."

"Back off, Bruiser," Peter said, before Brett could introduce her eldest bro to an old-fashioned gun-butt sandwich. "You might get a chance later, if little sister proves as useless as she used to be." He circled Brett, his fingers steepled together to point at Brett. "So tell me, little Brett, what can you do for us?"

Brett was so squicked by how icky Peter was, she realized she could stand up to Mark better. Mark was a big lug, but Peter was . . . Peter was . . . Ick. "I sometimes look into shit, and make sense of the nonsensical. I figure out who's done what and why, and why they might do even more shit. I know people, and I know shit. I've looked into this type of crap before and helped collar a bunch of murderers."

"So that tells me what, but the bigger question remains: Why?" Peter had truly foul breath. He'd always had it, Brett remembered. It was about as bad as their dad's had been and it still made her want to throw up—it was an automatic gag reflex.

"A few women think I ought to do it. They might forgive me some . . . er . . . *transgressions* . . . if I do."

92

Peter stopped his vulturic circling. "So little sister has grown up to be a Higgins after all."

"I lived under another name for a few years, because I wanted nothing to do with you all," Brett said. "But I came back to myself—my own name—to shove your noses in all I was, and all you weren't."

"You think you're hot shit or something?" Mark said, stepping up to Brett and ignoring Peter's gestures to stand still.

"I don't think it, I am." This banter made Brett feel better. She was familiar with this type of crap, and so Mark's actions put her at ease. She knew that even in hand-to-hand battle, she could now best him.

"You're the same little girl I f—"

Brett didn't give Mark a chance to finish his sentence. She grabbed him by the back of the neck and threw him face first into the ground. She pulled her gun again and held it to his temple. "Finish that sentence! I fuckin' dare ya to!"

"Oh, no," Peter said, crouching over Mark behind Brett, practically spooning her. "You don't want to do that. That's a Go to Jail card. Go directly to jail, don't solve the crime, don't save your family—and more importantly, don't get the girl back. Just . . . spend the rest of your life in jail. Not so appealing now, is it, little sister?" He ground his dick into her backside.

Brett twisted around, flipping off Mark and kicking Peter away in one move. She landed on her back, pointing her gun around at her brothers. "What the fuck do you sick freaks want from me?"

Peter stood. "Nothing, little sister. You came here, after all."

"What the fuck is your issue, bitch?" Mark said, lumbering to his feet to tower over her. "Don't go pointing that gun at me like you're shit, 'cause you ain't. You ain't now, you weren't then, and you never will be shit. Ya got that, bitch?"

"Mark," Peter said, a harsh note of command in his voice. "Go over to Bri's. Watch some football."

"Ain't no football on right now," Mark said.

"Go to Brian's. Watch sports, jack each other off, I don't care. Smash beer cans on your heads and get drunk. Whatever. Just go. Now," Peter commanded.

"What's goin' on, bro?"

"I need to talk with Brett. And you need to go. She does not particularly care for either of us, but you're being your obnoxious self, so you need to leave. After all, at some point, I won't be able to stop her from blowing your head—or dick—off."

"I'll be back in a coupla hours—whether she's still here or not!" Mark said, leaving.

Brett knew he'd listen to whatever Peter said. She hated them both but also realized that somehow the whiney, snivelly, littler, younger Peter had control over Mark. She wondered why.

"Let's go inside," Peter said.

"Why?"

"So we can talk. You're now bigger, stronger and better armed than I. If anybody's gonna get hurt, it's me. But you're not out for that, or else I'd be dead already. So I'm out to help you. After all, you're looking to help me, aren't you?" Peter led her inside, into the kitchen.

"Not of my own choosing. I'd like to see you all as worm food."

"Aww, the same old Brett—doing whatever anybody around you wants you to. You were always such a nice little girl. Compliant. Malleable. With a good mouth."

Brett backhanded him so hard he flew into the wall.

Peter brought himself to his feet. "Oh, so you've learned to stand up for yourself. You've got quite an arm there, lil' sis. And picking on smaller people? Guess we taught you right after all." He rubbed his jaw.

And Brett realized she was becoming a true Higgins. And she didn't like it one bit. "I'm here to help you. If you don't want me to, I can leave."

"Oh, hey, I like living," Peter said. "And I think you're the one who can help me continue doing so. I got Mark to leave, remember? So we could talk?"

"So then, talk. Tell me what you think I need to know." Brett leaned against the kitchen table, still towering over Peter.

"Somebody's killing our family. First Dad, then cousin Robert, cousin Steve, then Matthew. And then Timothy, Frank and John. It's too much to be coincidence."

Brett pulled out a notepad to jot down all the names, including the new ones. She didn't want to engage Peter in too long of a conversation, though, so she decided to go about it all as more of a fact-finding mission wherein she could discover more details on her own, or from others, later. "Why do you think they're connected?"

"Oh, Brett. Brett, Brett, Brett. There's no such thing as coincidence. For instance, why do you think you were born into this family?"

"Bad luck. So there's nothing beyond the sudden deaths of relatives that's making you think there's something going on?"

"There's no such thing as coincidence. And the death rate among our relatives seems to have skyrocketed. Especially among those who aren't at a high-mortality age. I could overlook those with other high-risk factors, but the bulk of evidence points to something else."

"Now, I can see why someone would want to off you all, but can you?"

Peter used his middle finger to push his glasses up his nose. "We're not exactly what most of the world would consider nice people. You're the only one worth much of anything, so whoever's doing this couldn't be after any money—or else they would've gone directly to you."

"So who do you propose is responsible? And why?" Brett made sure to remain standing, so she kept the height advantage over Peter. He'd seemed much taller when she was younger.

"Well, I would think it's somebody with something against us. All of us. Us being the males of the clan, that is. And, of course, it would have to be somebody capable of murder. Of killing. Of taking another life."

"So where are you going with this?"

"You're my number-one suspect."

"And I'm here investigating this because . . . ?"

"Laura asked you to, and you're doing it to cover yourself. Cover your tracks. Try to show your innocence." He strolled about the kitchen, keeping an eye on her as he touched various items—a newspaper, the microwave, a coffee cup.

Brett watched him, but didn't say a word.

He finally came to rest, leaning against the counter, to look at her. "I like it. But that's not what's going on, is it?"

"If I were killing you all, I'd want credit for it."

"Yes. I figured as much. You see, even when you were supposed to be dead, you had to make sure everyone eventually knew all about how good you were being." He stepped right up to Brett and tapped the newspaper sitting next to her on the kitchen table. "I read the newspapers, after all." He turned from her to grab a half gallon of juice from the fridge. "So it's not you. Just somebody else who has something against us. The list could, quite frankly, be endless." He poured his OJ into a glass and leaned back to slowly sip from it.

"So," Brett said, "bottom line, you don't know jack."

"Nothing more than you likely know. Down to how we're so small-time, this can't possibly be any sort of gang war."

"Yeah. You don't matter."

"You're right there."

"And if it were, I'd know about it. So . . ." Brett said. "You and Mark live together."

"He's a moron. As you likely know. But he's a roommate I know what to expect from."

"So tell me, Peter, what is it you do these days? You know all

96

about me, yet I know nothing about you."

"I do taxes," he said. Brett wanted to do an "I-told-you-so" dance, 'cause she'd *so* had him pegged. "As our brothers got older, I had to learn some things about the law and taxes to help keep them out of jail as much as possible. And since I'm the runt of the litter, I couldn't use my size like the rest of you to aid me in my pursuit of a living. I couldn't be all rough and tough and towering malicious."

"You did enough of that when we were younger."

"Oh, yes. I remember the good old days with you."

Brett wanted to kill him right there and then.

"I guess I can't look forward to any reprisals of such, little sister."

"Do you realize," Brett said, "I could kill you both in cold blood and never serve a single day? I have friends, and we know how to hide bodies so nobody ever finds them."

Chapter Ten

Brett had stopped by the theater long enough to make sure everything was running okay, and get some more addresses to check out. She wanted to talk to all the immediate survivors of all the killings thus far. Who knew—talking with Peter had already expanded the number of related deaths, so more talk could lead to further leads.

Brett went up to Warren, wanting to get away from Frankie and all the rest of her friends, as well as Allie and anyone else. She needed a nice, quiet place to think—but not too quiet. She didn't want it so quiet that she might think about Allie, or remember any of the amazing times they'd had together.

She wanted to focus on the case at hand.

Jesus H. Christ, what the hell was she thinking about? Thinking of this as a case? Was she becoming some sort of a private dick or shit? Hell, that was the last thing she needed. Only dick she had she kept in a drawer in the bedside table. Well, unless of course she was packing it.

So she needed a quiet place, or not-so-quiet place to think.

"Brett! How the hell ya doing?" Jeff said, walking up to her and slapping her shoulder, guiding her to a table.

"Hanging in, Jeff."

"Burger and a beer for my friend here," Jeff said, pointing to one of the topless waitresses. Charlie's was well known for its *Businessman's Luncheons*. Jeff's dad was the one who opened the joint, and then Jeff and his brother took it over after their dad died—that is, until Jeff's bro bit it in a hit-and-run *accident*. Now Jeff ran it. Like he ran a few other joints around the edges of Detroit.

No matter how cheesy and tasteless this topless joint was, it was like the Ritz compared to Brett and Frankie's Paradise Theater. At least one holdover from the days when first his dad, then he and his bro, ran the joint was that Brett, with some help from her .357, had already earned his respect.

"So what brings you out this way?" Jeff asked.

"Just needed some room to think. Thanks, babe," she said to the half-naked blonde who put a cheddar bacon burger, medium well, fries, ranch dressing and a bottle of Miller Lite in front of her. Brett looked back over at the slender blond waitress in time to catch the woman wink at her.

Brett sat back, took a bite of her burger, a slug of her beer, smiled and winked back at the woman. She then laid her glare directly on Jeff. "I said I needed some room to think."

"Oh, yeah, sure. Well, y'know, give a yell if you need anything or anything. Y'know."

"Yeah, I know. Now get outta here and lemme think. And eat." She took another big bite of her burger and another slug of her beer, giving Jeff a thoroughly cold shoulder before she turned her attention to her notebook, where she'd put all her notes, including as much of a family tree as she'd been able to develop.

She knew who she'd given Frankie to look into so far, and knew who she'd have to go and talk to. The problem was, she didn't want to talk to—or see—*any* of her family.

She couldn't help but wish she'd come from a family that'd disowned her when she'd come out. 'Course, she'd gotten out before she'd come out, but that didn't make much of a difference.

She suddenly realized she should have Frankie get his folks to look into Luke and Laura's supposed ministry as well, so she finished her beer, waved the bottle at the waitress and pulled out her cell phone.

"Yeah, Frankie," she said into his voicemail. "I need you and your people to look into this ministry my brother Luke and his wife, Laura, supposedly run. Also, I want to make sure I gave you the names of *all* my brothers—Matthew, Mark, Luke, John, Peter and Paul—to look into. As well as all the dead folks. And all the families and connections thereof."

"Brett Higgins displaying an interest in her real family, will surprises never end?" Tina O'Rourke said, straddling a chair across from Brett.

"Tina. What an unpleasant surprise."

"You talking about your family, while here I always thought you crawled out from under a rock."

"I could only wish my family *had* abandoned me. They make me kinda jealous of turtles."

"Turtles?" Tina asked.

"*Their* parents abandon them at birth," Brett said, standing. "Now please excuse, I have to go visit a library to do some research. You know what libraries are, right? Big buildings with lots of books inside them?"

"You forget, I actually got an MBA before taking over the family business, unlike some people, who only have a bachelor's. And not just any ol' family business to speak of—the sort they make movies and TV shows about."

"Still don't mean you know how to read or what a library is." Brett walked out, not bothering to look behind her to see what, if anything, Tina did, or whom she might've talked with.

Brett was in her car, driving while trying to decide which library to go to—Detroit Public, Wayne State, or a local Warren one, when she questioned her reasoning. How was she planning on looking up her relatives at the library? Wouldn't it be better if she simply went home and looked 'em all up online in the comfort of her own home, with perhaps a nice Scotch at her side?

After all, she only wanted to work up a family tree. She'd met a bunch of her family when she was younger because, obviously, they were total white trash, but she'd tried to forget about all of that and, through the many intervening years, she'd been amazingly unsuccessful at it. So she already knew who a bunch of her relatives were—definitely enough to give her a nice, good, solid starting place for her family-tree researching.

She guessed she'd look up births and deaths and all that in the newspapers, but there were likely also a lot of genealogy sites on the Web. She was sure there had to be such things, even though she'd never had any interest in looking them up herself. Her family sucked, so why would she ever want to find any more of them, except maybe to kill 'em herself?

But by the time she'd worked all that out, she was already at the Wilder Branch of the Detroit Public Library. She might as well go in and talk to someone. Maybe talking with someone might help her figure out what she ought to do and how to go about it. A good reference librarian might be able to help her work out a family tree on her dad's side of the family. She didn't care about her mom's at all.

She'd already figured out that everybody who was getting it was from her dad's side—they were the ones who lived with entitlement and the entire world-done-me-wrong mentality. Even as they fucked with everybody else, they thought they deserved more.

She entered the library and looked around. There was a woman with her two screaming kids, and another woman with three well-behaved kids. She remembered herself and her mom when she was growing up; none of the moms here even vaguely resembled them.

Brett couldn't take any more of this crap. It didn't matter what any librarian could tell or teach her, she needed to get away.

Of course, as she left, she spotted a little brochure: *How to track down your family on the Web.* Goddamned everything was on the Web now. She could probably find directions for taking out her entire family on the Web. Probably find people willing to do it for her there, too. The World Wide Weapon. The trouble was, if she wanted to start taking 'em out, she'd want the fun and gratification of doing it herself.

As she drove home, she developed her plan of attack. She'd make her family tree. She knew about her mom and dad and brothers, and that Paul married Chriss and they had two kids. And that so far, Dad, then cousin Robert, cousin Steve, then Matthew, and then Timothy, Frank and John had bought it. Well, okay, so that was sum total of all who were dead from this supposed serial killer. She didn't know the order for sure, but she did need to figure that out. And she needed to determine if these were murders and, if so, if they were related.

She'd spoken with her mother, Mark, Paul and Peter. She guessed she should've interrogated Paul, Chriss, their kids, and John's widow and sons more, but she couldn't do any of that today. She'd seen them yesterday and wasn't up to it again so soon.

She needed to look online, do some investigating that way. Talk to everyone connected to anyone who'd died—so pretty much, her dad's entire side of the family—and figure out the connections. There had to be some connection between everyone who was biting it, and since the murderer—if there was one, and it wasn't just freak coincidence and an incredibly strong stupid streak in her patriarchal lineage—was running amok in her own family, there were already built-in connections. Everybody was connected.

She was sure that the key lay in motive—but hell, even she had a reason to kill all these guys, so she could only assume motives abounded. They all done somebody wrong and pissed more than a few folks off enough to get themselves killed.

Again, why should she care? Especially since all it was doing was causing fights between her and Allie and Victoria, bringing back lots of bad memories, and making her life a living hell?

She called up Luke's church, the Ministry of the Healing Hand. It had a nice and professional Web site, and she saw that it had gotten a bit of publicity for all the donations it made. There was even a Healing Hand Foundation, to channel parishioners' donations into supposedly good causes.

Brett called the church office. "I'm from the *Roanoke Record*," she told the woman who answered the phone, "and I'm doing an article on a new church in these parts that says it's modeled after Michigan's Ministry of the Healing Hand."

"Yes, that's us," the woman volunteered, which was a prime example of a *duh* moment, since she'd answered the phone saying, "Ministry of the Healing Hand, how may I direct your call?"

"Yes, that's what I thought when I called you," Brett said, taking a sip of her Scotch and flipping through the church's Web site, which had enough pictures of her brother Luke to make her have to take a few more Tums. She'd have to get some more of those with how this case was turning her stomach. "I was wondering if you could tell me a little about the church and its founder"—she flipped the pages of her notebook, so it'd sound like she was looking it up—"Mr. Luke Higgins?"

"Oh, Brother Higgins is simply marvelous and truly has an inspiring story. He has one of the most amazing rags-to-riches stories I've ever heard. Not that he's rich, by any means. He makes sure that all the money raised by the church goes into the community and the world. He's always coming to the board with grant proposals from underserved people and communities here and abroad."

"Could you tell me about some of them?"

"He's helped establish a business in South Africa that gives locals small, one-time loans to start businesses. For instance, people might want to become weavers and they need money to buy the initial wool and the loom. So they get a loan, which they repay with interest, and then they're self-sufficient. We continue helping because sometimes, they'll ship us some of their items as gifts, and we resell them—or auction them off, since you can make a lot more through an auction than an outright sale, especially when people know they're supporting a good cause by bidding, or buying raffle tickets—at the church."

Brett didn't know enough about enough to try to figure out if this loan thing was true, but she did quickly find on the Web, even as they spoke, agencies that did in fact provide the exact sort of small start-up loans in underprivileged countries that this woman talked about.

There was a chance Luke and his church and all that were legit. But she wasn't holding her breath on it. "Wow," she finally said, realizing the woman was waiting for some sort of response, "that does sound truly inspirational." She tried her best to keep her voice amazed.

"I could fax or e-mail you one-sheets on all of our current fundings," the woman offered. She dropped the words as if they'd only recently been placed into her vocabulary. Brett could imagine her as some little old lady with too much time and money on her hands, volunteering such wherever she could justify it.

"That'd be great," Brett said, quickly setting up a new Gmail account under RoanokeRecordReporter@gmail.com. Fortunately, the handle wasn't yet taken by anyone.

"I have to ask," the woman said, as she apparently jotted the address down. "Is this the Roanoke I learned about in history?"

"Yeah," Brett said, not quite sure herself. "The vanishing colony and all that. Listen, myself and a colleague are going up to Michigan soon on another story. Would you mind terribly if we stopped by to meet with you?"

"Oh, definitely. We always love showing our church to others!"

Brett already knew the congregation was located in West Bloomfield which, although not quite as affluent as Bloomfield proper, wasn't exactly one of Detroit's poor neighbors. From what she'd seen online, people came in from a wide area, none of which was Detroit, but all of which had the potential for some wealthy clientele.

She still wasn't sure of Laura's veracity on the matter of Luke and her money and where it all went.

"Great, then how about if we see you at about eleven on Thursday?"

"That would be wonderful! I'll be here, you know. I volunteer here six days a week—"

Brett wanted to dance. She'd known this was a volunteer and not a paid secretary.

"But I didn't catch your name, dear?"

"Victoria. Victoria Nelson," Brett said, knowing that to get anywhere with this woman she'd have to have Victoria come with her to charm her properly. Maybe even send her by herself. "And whom should I ask for?"

"Oh, sorry, how rude of me. My name's Helen. Helen

Anderson."

Brett hung up feeling one step closer to debunking the frauds that surrounded her family. She immediately called Victoria to let her know what she needed her to do. Victoria decided that Brett would come with her, posing as a male friend of some sort, since, as Victoria put it, "If you've got her right, she won't think twice about you being male."

By the time they got off the phone, Helen had e-mailed Brett the funding information she'd promised—including information both on where their money came from and where it went. Brett immediately noticed her brother Peter's name listed as the accountant, and she assumed the firm that conducted the audit was a one-man firm he'd established to make it look as if he was a legitimate accounting firm or auditor.

She noticed that a number of donations to the church were from people who wished to remain anonymous, and many of the donations and gifts the church made were to actual things that didn't list the church as a funder—although they all did list something either close to the church's name or anonymous gifts. A lot of places the church supposedly gave gifts to she couldn't find on the Net, but, of course, they were apparently sold to the congregation as too small and remote to be listed on the Web—like little places in South America, Asia and Africa.

Looked like a lot of Enronitis double-playing with the money to her, as well as a good dose of money laundering added in for kicks.

By the time Brett turned off her office lights for the night, she felt a lot better. She not only knew a lot more and had a game plan, but she hadn't thought about her family beyond the circumstances of the investigation for hours, not even Merry.

Still, she went outside to her SUV, taking a moment to pet the big yellow Lab that came running over to her from her neighbor's house. She was amazed that that neighbor hadn't told his dog her yard was off-limits, since he had seen her gun more than once, and each time it seemed to unnerve him even more. Allie'd always been the one to make nice with the neighbors. The neighborhood Brett had grown up in was overrun with guns, and her last few neighborhoods before she and Allie moved here hadn't been much better.

Brett was used to guns, what with her line of business and where she'd grown up and all the other reasons. Allie wasn't too put off by them since she was a cop, came from a bunch of cops (though her dad wasn't one, nor her mother, for that matter) and had always wanted to be a cop. Granted, she had been shocked the first time she'd seen Brett pull a gun on a guy, but that was in her high school, so her shock and dismay were understandable.

Brett realized her own high school reunion would be coming up. Allie had a blast at her last one, but Brett didn't reckon her high school could even track her down anymore. Plus, she didn't feature going back to that, since she'd worked so hard to get away from it all.

She drove by Rowan's house, driving slowly around the entire block before pulling into the empty, for-sale house directly behind Rowan's so she could stroll through the yard and hop the fence into Rowan's backyard. From there, it didn't take very long at all for her to get into the house. No matter how much trouble she'd been in in the past, Rowan really was so cocky as to figure that her standing as a cop was enough to keep any burglars out. Little did she think that anyone would break in not to steal, but just to look around.

Of course, before she entered, Brett pulled on the latex gloves she'd started keeping in her jackets and coats. There was never any telling when she'd have to get sneaky about something and need to hide her whereabouts, and whether or not she'd been somewhere in particular. She quickly found the guest bedroom where Allie was staying and was vindicated in everything once she discovered that Allie was keeping a picture of her on the bedside table.

If she knew Allie at all, she knew that sometimes that picture was turned down or put into a drawer—but still, Allie was keeping a framed picture of her near, which was good.

Rowan wasn't much of a cook. The lack of culinary equipment attested to that—as did the number of frozen dinners in the freezer. Rowan actually seemed to have headed into a pretty solitary life once she'd moved in here—she had the DVDs and CDs and Wii and all that to show how she spent much of her spare time.

Allie's boxes were in Rowan's basement, where not much else lived, not even old storage or power equipment. Rowan didn't seem to do much or have much else. She was like a two-dimensional character, and Brett knew Allie could do a lot—big, great big loads lots—better.

And then Brett went up to the master bedroom and went through Rowan's things. One thing became immediately apparent, and that was that Rowan didn't have much of a sense of style. Her clothes were humdrum and predictable. No wonder she was still a beat cop. There wasn't much to her, nothing to suggest that she could do any more with her life, that was for sure.

When Brett opened Rowan's bedside table she found a picture of Allie. And then, to trump that, the sound of a car on the street broke into her consciousness and broke her train of thought. But she didn't think too much about it, since Allie was in class and Rowan was at work and Brett knew both their schedules well enough to be sure about this. So she took her time going through the drawer and looking around until she found a second and a third photo of Allie—pictures from when she and Rowan worked together, and then when Brett and Allie helped Rowan, and some from even after that.

That was about when the car door slammed. And also when Brett got truly pissed about finding a picture of Allie sleeping.

Rowan was totally invading Allie's space. Brett could bust her on this alone—bust her as in bust her jaw, or bust her with Allie, but she had to calm down 'cause she didn't want to blow it all on a single round.

She wanted all the bananas.

It was when Brett, on a strange urge, reached under Rowan's pillow and found yet another picture—a scented picture, for fuck's sake—that she heard the front door open.

Allie should've been in class and Rowan should've been at work, which was why Brett didn't worry too much when she'd heard the car. Now she got worried. Worried with a capital *W*.

She looked out the window and saw Allie's car but realized she already knew it was Allie since she recognized the sounds of Allie coming in—her keys as she walked, her keys in the lock, her tread, her taking off her jacket . . . everything. She was confident she knew what Allie looked like and what she smelled like, but she had no idea that she knew so well how Allie *sounded*. She did, apparently.

She knew her woman, and knew her well. Rowan didn't. Rowan likely held Allie in some sort of a gilded cage, or on a pedestal or whatever clichéd phrase all the cool kids were using this year. Rowan'd be shocked to know how nasty and dirty Allie could be, and how, sometimes, she liked to be fucked hard and fast.

For fuck's sake, Rowan didn't even own a decent dildo or harness, though she had a coupla vibrators, which she likely used only on herself. Brett knew she didn't have anything to worry about, but she still didn't like the idea of Rowan having her hands all over her Allie. Or convincing Allie that she was something other than what she was.

She wanted the winning and losing to be fair and square.

And now Allie was hopping into a shower downstairs. That actually wasn't like Allie. Allie showered in the morning and before special events at night—like if she and Brett had a hot date.

Brett wondered if Allie had some sort of a hot date that night.

109

Brett reached inside her jacket to fondle her .357. She thought again that she needed to trade in the trustworthy firearm since, recently, she'd gotten the drop on some joker who tried taking out a dancer at the theater because the kid had a single- or double-action gun with a hammer in his pants, and the hammer'd gotten stuck on the waistband of his jeans when he'd pulled it out. Brett realized that one of these days that sort of thing might happen to her, so it'd be good if she traded guns to something that made that sort of thing impossible.

But old habits were hard to break, and this gun was like a part of herself, even though she had quite a few others at her disposal.

But none of that mattered right now, not even how badly Brett wanted to sabotage Rowan's guns, ammunition or anything else, since that sort of thing might get her killed. Although Brett didn't see the bad in that, she knew she shouldn't, so she didn't.

Besides, right now it was more important for her to think about how the hell to get out of the house. One of the stairs had squeaked something awful when she came upstairs, so she didn't want to go back down them. She couldn't very well go out the front window but . . . she walked over to Rowan's bathroom and realized that she could probably get out that way. To be sure she glanced out all the windows and then opened the back one as the shower stopped, making her glad she hadn't gone down the stairs because, since the shower was so short, she likely would've been caught in the act of opening the door to leave by Allie.

Instead, she slipped out the window, doing a severe pull-up so she could pull it shut behind her as she hung from the ledge, then let herself down as far as she could go by hanging, until she dropped down to the ground, pretty damned silently, she thought.

She slipped over the back fence and out to her car, totally not caught, or at least she thought.

En route home Brett drove by first Luke and Laura's house, then Luke's church. At both places she circled and took pictures with the digital camera she'd bought a few years back to take pictures of the dancers.

Back in Rick's day they took pictures of the dancers with an old Polaroid Instamatic, or whatever the hell the thing was called. That way they could immediately post the pictures, with the dancers' names, in the lobby, so the guys could see who all was dancing each week, or weekend, as the case might be.

With the digital camera, Brett could print the pictures a bit bigger and have them on file, in case any pics went missing in between times.

Same old, only updated.

Now she used that same technology so she could look at the places after the fact to see how she might break into each, if it came down to that, and to show Victoria, so she could have some idea of what they were walking into.

After all, it was always good to know the shit you were getting into in advance, at least to the best of your abilities.

She then stopped by a store to pick up some more technology, then headed on, all without actually thinking the words "casing the joint." At least, she didn't allow them to herself yet.

Chapter Eleven

She'd done her research, her reconnaissance, and now she reckoned she could either go on to interrogations or surveillance, or she could do something more interesting, like break into the church, Luke and Laura's home, or else find out why Allie cut class.

The latter was obviously by far the most important, so Brett got right on it. First she stopped by the house to print out all the pictures she'd taken earlier, and to shower, put on clean clothes and cologne, and then she went off to Rowan's. Unfortunately, Rowan would be home by now, but that was okay. Rowan and Allie kept coming at her, so now it was time to return the favor.

But by the time she got to Rowan's, Allie was gone. Or at least her car was. Rowan was home, however, so Brett decided to avail herself of the chance to assail her competition. One couldn't always take the high road. This time she definitely felt like taking the low road. Rowan should be glad she wasn't going subterranean. She'd keep it terranean, if for no other reason than it'd piss Allie off if she didn't.

So she went up to the front door and knocked, like a civilized sort of individual, and Rowan, either still feeling cocky 'cause she was a goddamned cop, or else pissed off since Allie wasn't waiting for her with a turkey pot pie when she got home, opened the door immediately, without first checking to see who it was. Regardless, she was definitely *not* expecting Brett when she opened the door, that much was immediately apparent when she tried to slam the door on Brett.

Tried of course being the operative word.

"Yo, Rowan, babe, what's up?" Brett said, walking in.

"Allie's not here," Rowan said.

"And that's kinda pissing you off, ain't it?"

"No. Allie does whatever she wants. I'm only giving her a place to stay."

"Yeah, right," Brett said, tossing her trench onto the sofa, going into the kitchen and finding a beer in the fridge. "So you got any idea where she's at?"

"Nope. None at all."

"Does she have a class now?"

"Don't know, don't care."

"Really? Why don't you tell me another one." Brett made herself at home in the living room.

"What the hell do you think you're doing?"

"Evening things up a bit. You keep coming 'round mine these days and I figured I'd return the favor."

"I come over to yours—your house—when I'm with Allie."

"Whatever. I wanted to check out your digs for a change." She got up and wandered around the main floor. "So I s'pose this is the guest room, and this is the bathroom? You got a study somewhere?"

"Over—what the hell business of yours is it?"

"It's mine 'cause my girlfriend's living with you right now. Your bedroom upstairs?" Brett opened the door leading up and ran up the stairs before Rowan could stop her.

"This is *not* cool, Higgins," Rowan said, following her.

"Yeah, but it's getting you where you live," Brett said, opening the closet. "And evening things up." Brett turned around, brushed Rowan away and went to her bed, where she flopped down. "So I guess this is where you lie at night, fantasizing about my girl, huh?"

"That's none of your damned business!"

"Yes, it is, 'cause she's mine and she's gonna stay mine and your life's gonna get even more fucked if you even think about fucking her." Brett stood, looked Rowan right in the eye, then turned and opened the drawer. "Yeah, try telling me you don't play with yourself at night thinking about her," she said, tossing the pictures on the bed.

"I'm a cop! You can't break in here—"

"I didn't break in here. You opened the door. You haven't asked me to leave."

"Leave!"

"Oooo, who's trying to grow a pair now? Know this, Abernathy, you mess with me and you won't do it again. Ever."

"Did you just threaten a cop?"

"Nope. Not at all. I was telling it like it is. Now I'm gonna go chat with my girl, and I'd suggest that you stop even trying to get with someone so far above you."

It was only when Brett turned the ignition and took off that she allowed herself to tell herself that she didn't do that to let Rowan know who was in charge, nor to make sure her prints were all over the house, in case she had to go back, nor to make sure Rowan stayed in her place. She did it 'cause it was fun and she needed some fun these days—and she needed times of knowing she was in charge and she could still put others in their places. She needed it like a drug *and* she needed it so she could feel better about everything spinning out of control in her life.

She liked this feeling a lot more.

Brett then drove over to Twelve Mile High, aka Macomb County Community College. Allie already had a bachelor's degree in criminal science, but now she was taking classes. Brett wasn't sure what all classes she was taking, but she knew some were women's studies and other things that made her question Brett and what Brett did for a living and all of that.

If Allie hadn't cut class earlier, she should've been in class now, or just out of it, so Brett cruised the area and saw Allie in a heated convo with someone—maybe a classmate or a prof—out by her car.

Brett continued cruising the area, keeping a bit of an eye on Allie and trying not to be spotted or noticed, while trying also not to lose sight or track of her. Another woman joined Allie and the other woman, and the three of them took off at the same time.

And they all went to the same place. A little bar down the street. Brett continued cruising by, wishing she'd thought to borrow someone else's car when Allie started paying attention to her. She knew if she continued this she'd have to start using other vehicles. After all, Allie wasn't just anyone, she was an ex-cop and so might notice things more than most.

Hell, she *would* notice things more than most. Brett had to remember that her girl was nobody's fool and she'd pick up on things and get mighty pissed off when she did.

But still, Brett parked in a lot near the bar, slipped into the bar's lot, slid by Allie's car and went along into the bar.

Brett knew she didn't blend too well. She was more built to intimidate. She was tall—five-eleven—and when folks figured out she was a woman, that alone could draw their attention. She was used to using her size, dress and bearing to ensure that nobody fucked with her, and that tended to draw attention to her. Generally, she didn't mind it, even when she used it only to help her pick up women.

Now it worked against her. But still she tried to be nonchalant as she sidled into the bar, got a beer and tried to blend.

She blended like . . . something that didn't blend at all well. It was more like putting a magnet next to another magnet of equal attraction, so the two split like a banana. Once Brett realized how bad it was, she thought about splitting, but it was already too late. Allie'd spotted her.

"What the fuck do you think you're doing?" Allie asked, grabbing her by the collar and pulling her to the side of the bar.

"Getting a drink." Sometimes, even when she didn't mean to, Brett seemed confrontational. About as *sometimes* as raccoons dig through trash, but still, it *sometimes* wasn't *meant* to be.

"Not buying it. What are you doing here?"

"Right now I've gotten a drink and am drinking it."

"And before?"

Brett obfuscated. "You weren't home, so I wanted to make sure you were all right."

"I'm fine. So go."

"Once I finish this."

"Finish it now, then."

"What the fuck, Sullivan?"

"You're following me, *Higgins*. I saw your SUV go by, repeatedly, and now you're in here. It doesn't take a genius to realize that two plus two plus two equals six."

"You're getting to be a real bitch, Allie."

"I'm the woman you made me, Brett."

Brett wanted to pull Allie into her arms and hold her all night . . . hold her . . . forever. And she wished she could tell her that. But she couldn't. Even if she could, Allie wouldn't listen. Not now, not tonight. Brett needed to do something, make herself something, put the pieces together so she *could* tell her that.

For now she put down her beer and left.

She was opening the door to her SUV when she felt someone come up beside her, and by the time Allie put a hand on her forearm she would've decked her except that she knew her sounds and her smell and . . . *dear God, I can even recognize her touch*, Brett thought. So she stopped herself from decking Allie and instead covered Allie's hand with her own.

"How's the investigation going?" Allie asked.

"It's going. I'm running it by the numbers—y'know, looking into it all," Brett said, as coolly and calmly as she could. "I'm gonna go visit Luke's church tomorrow."

"So there really is a church?"

"Appears so. I checked 'em out on the Web, then called and spoke to someone. That sort of thing."

"Do you need backup?"

Brett was ready to tell her that she was going to go in with Victoria, then she re-engaged her brain. "If you're offering, I can use you. I don't seem to play well with the church ladies," she said, scuffing the toe of her boot against the ground and looking up at Allie while her head was down. She knew damned well it was a clichéd move, but it worked for a reason, and so she used it.

It took Allie a moment before she responded, "What do you need?"

"I told the volunteer secretary or whatever that I was with a newspaper doing a story on a local church that was based on Luke's and I'd be in town tomorrow, so could I look around and maybe talk to some folks."

"So where are you supposed to be from?" Allie's hand still burned through Brett's trench down to her forearm.

"Roanoke."

"That's Virginia, right?"

"Damned if I know. I only said what came to mind."

"Brett! You have to think these things through!"

"Yeah, yeah, I thought about that when she asked if we were the lost colony and all that."

"What am I gonna do with you?"

"Love me."

Allie paused. Long enough for Brett to slide her hand down to meet Allie's and hold Allie's for a moment.

"We'll see," Allie finally said before releasing Brett's hand. Then she whispered, "You should ask Laura about Merry, y'know," turned and walked away.

Brett was happy that she turned to look back at the last moment to catch Allie watching her drive out of the lot.

Brett got home and wanted to bask in the Allieness of the evening. She wanted to remember the sounds and smells and feelings of Allie. She wanted to remember what she felt like.

She didn't want to lose her or that, any or all of that. Ever.

But then Victoria called. And Brett wasn't tired nor ready for sleep yet. She was sitting up and playing Godfather: Blackhand Edition on her Wii and drinking. She liked blowing the heads off the bad guys and having to flail around herself when she was beating the crap outta them.

Brett told Victoria if she was gonna stop by, she'd have to park down the street.

"I'm trying to help you and you want me to park down the street?"

"Yes."

"What the fuck, Brett? I sometimes don't know what's going on inside that skull of yours."

"Y'know, Victoria, you making this much of a deal about where you park is telling me that you care less about me and more about making sure Allie sees you here and knows you're here, and that don't impress me much." Brett had muted and paused the game when Victoria called, and now she unpaused it but left it muted so she could continue to play while talking with Victoria. "So why don't you just go on home tonight." Brett hung up and went back to her game. Since Allie'd left she'd realized she could more easily hold her temper during potentially volatile phone convos if she played her game while talking. It took her focus away from the convo, so she couldn't get so intensely involved with it. Wii was a barrier of dispassion to her at times.

Someone came knocking at her door. She glanced up, paused the game, grabbed her gun, checked the peephole and opened the door. "Victoria. I didn't expect you."

"No, of course not, you told me to go home." Victoria came in, tossed her purse and a backpack onto the sofa, pulled her coat off, dropped it on the kitchen table, went to the fridge, pulled out a Diet Pepsi, and sat on the arm of the couch next to where Brett sat when she turned her game back on.

Brett played. Victoria walked over and looked at the other games Brett had, being careful not to step between Brett and the TV screen.

"Damnit!" Brett yelled, throwing the controls down when she died again.

"Okay, so how do you do this?" Victoria said, picking them up.

"Well, you shoot and you take over businesses and kill the bad guys, try not to kill any innocents or cops . . ."

"No, I mean"—Victoria held the controls the way Brett had been holding them and figured out how to get the game to continue—"what was up with you being all like you were in a real fight and all that?"

"Well, the sensor on top of the TV sees how you're moving things, so you actually gotta knock some of the guys upside the head and all that."

"Oh. Okay."

Brett did briefly wonder if Allie was gonna come in and catch them working and playing together like this, and then she thought, "Fuck it."

"So what have you figured out?" Victoria eventually asked. Obviously unbeknownst to Brett, she'd been trying to figure out how to get Brett to wrap her arms around her to show her how to use things. This hadn't worked, so she was trying to build camaraderie and such with Brett.

"Not a helluva lot," Brett said.

"You got any games we can play together?"

Brett turned to Victoria, briefly imagining her to be Storm, her older sister, and pausing before she said, "I'd have to look." She was thinking of other sorts of games the two of them could play together.

"So what have you done?"

"I've worked out some more folks who died, likely in the same serial. I'm trying to get more info on those cases, so I can work out the methods and causes of death and all that crap."

"What do you mean *methods and causes*?"

"Well, I mean one dude maybe might've ODed on heroin, but was it an accident—like, didn't he know he'd just taken a dose, or maybe this cut was stronger than he was used to, or did someone tie him down and shove it into him, or did he do it as an intentional suicide? I don't know all the words and terms and shit, but you got what you know after, and then you have to try to figure out how it happened."

"So are you saying some of these people ran themselves over or shot themselves?"

Brett stopped. She reached over and hit the pause button. "You know more than you're letting on." There was no way Victoria should know that one did indeed die of a gunshot and another got ran over.

"I always know more than you think, Brett," Victoria said, turning the game back on and slamming the guy who'd killed Brett. A prostitute dressed in a scrap of lingerie came up to her onscreen persona and Victoria was offered a few options. "Well, she's *so* not my type," she said, deciding not to flirt with the woman, who immediately gave her information on how to blackmail the chief of police.

Brett sidled up to Victoria. "But you *are* my type." She slipped her arms around Victoria's slender waist and nuzzled her ear and neck.

"Tell me, Brett," Victoria said, still playing the game. "Did you ask me to park down the street in case Allie stopped by tonight or because you knew you'd want me to spend the night?"

"No. But that doesn't mean I don't want you to."

"So you treat me like this and expect me to spend the night with you?"

"No." Brett reached down, picked Victoria up and carried her upstairs.

"B-B-Brett," Victoria said as Brett laid her onto her bed, "what are you doing?"

"Making love to you," Brett said, not quite lying on Victoria and kissing down Victoria's neck to her collarbone.

Victoria's hands were on Brett's shoulders, clutching the fabric of Brett's shirt as if she couldn't make up her mind whether to draw her toward her or push her away. "Brett . . ."

"Do you want me to stop?" Brett asked, not stopping, but instead running her tongue across Victoria's collarbone.

"God no."

"Then let it go." Brett lay down on top of Victoria, sliding her leg between Victoria's and pressing down against Victoria's heat. She raised up on her forearms and ran her tongue lightly across Victoria's lips, nibbled on them until Victoria groaned and opened her mouth to Brett, letting Brett enter her with her tongue.

Brett leaned down, teasing Victoria with a give-and-take play of mouths and lips, keeping the pressure on between Victoria's legs, pressing down on her there, making her arch up against her.

"God, please, Brett," Victoria said.

Brett rolled over to the side, so her hand could play over Victoria's breasts, down to where her sweater parted to allow access to her smooth and soft tummy. She kept leaning over so as to be able to keep kissing Victoria, even as her fingers swiftly undid the buttons on Victoria's light blue cardigan.

"Brett, this is the bed you share with Allie," Victoria said, moving against Brett regardless.

"She moved out on me." Brett reached directly into Victoria's bra to cup her breast.

"God, Brett." Victoria thrust upward, right against Brett.

"Do you want me to stop?" Brett said, not stopping, reaching behind Victoria to undo her bra. She helped Victoria sit upright so she could pull off the sweater and bra quickly and easily.

Brett kissed Victoria full on, then reached down to cup her breasts and run her hands over Victoria's naked breasts and torso before she helped her lie back down on her back with Brett on top of her.

Brett undid the zipper on her jeans, sliding it down before sliding them off Victoria, along with her silky panties and cotton socks. The lights were out, and it felt right to have them out now, this time, but still the moon's light coming through the blinds let her enjoy the beauty of Victoria's naked body, let her relish the wonderful lines, olive skin and bounteous breasts.

Aw, hell, she liked looking at the naked woman and thought she was fucking gorgeous, and just the sight of her made her wet and made her mouth water. Brett stripped off her own sweater, jeans and socks, then lay down again on top of Victoria.

"Brett, you know I like you naked," Victoria said, pulling at the hem of Brett's T-shirt. Brett sat up and pulled off her T and sports bra. "I'll let that slide," Victoria said, referring to Brett still wearing boxers. Probably because Brett had begun kissing her again like nobody's business.

Victoria wrapped her legs around Brett's hips, drawing her

into her. Victoria arched up into Brett. Brett ran her hands lightly all over Victoria, briefly cupping her breasts, caressing her nipples and hips, then delving between her legs, seeing how wet she was.

"Oh, God," Brett said, feeling the wetness and letting her fingers dip briefly into Victoria.

"Brett," Victoria said, moving against her.

"I love you," Brett said.

"I know," Victoria said.

Brett slid down Victoria's body, taking each nipple between first her lips, then her teeth, toying and playing and tugging and pulling, building up the tension, playing with one nipple with her mouth and teeth while she tugged and twisted and teased the other with her fingers, then vice versa.

She built it up and up with Victoria, enjoying the way the woman moaned and moved against her, then slowly moved down her body until she was between Victoria's legs, sliding her fingers up into her even as she breathed in her scent and began stroking up and down her clit with her tongue.

"Brett . . ." Victoria said.

Brett pulled out of Victoria.

"Please, God, don't stop," Victoria said.

"I'm not." Brett reached into the bedside drawer to grab a tube of lube. She liberally coated her hand with it, then slid two fingers into Victoria, then three . . .

"God, Brett . . ."

"Open your legs for me, baby," Brett said, returning to lapping up Victoria, running her tongue up and down Victoria, caressing her clit with her tongue . . .

. . . and sliding four fingers into her, moving them in and out and in and out until she added the thumb and pushed her fist slowly up into Victoria.

"Oh God oh God ohgodohgod Oh God!" Victoria writhed and pushed against her, thrashing about the bed so Brett had to

123

hold her hips down so as to not hurt her, to not slam in and out of her before she was ready . . . to instead slowly move around inside her, twisting her fist around as Victoria moved against her and opened her legs wide.

Brett's mouth was on Victoria, her fist inside her, and they moved together, against together and along with each other . . . Brett moving in and out, her tongue going up and down, Victoria moaning and groaning and begging . . .

"Brett, please, please . . ."

"What, make you come?"

"Make love to me."

It was a dorky cliché, but it fit the moment, so Brett didn't call her on it, or make fun of her for it.

Chapter Twelve
November 12

Victoria thought she was in heaven the next morning. Brett was again holding her, and had done so all night long. For one of the very few times in her life, Victoria felt loved and wanted and truly cherished.

She pulled Brett's arm tighter around her, knowing she was sleeping on Allie's side of the bed and she should feel guilty and that it was wrong, but she wanted to be loved and wanted and cherished, and it felt, right now, that she was.

And she knew she was.

And right now she could imagine that it was permanent and would be for always.

That was, until the phone rang and woke Brett up. Victoria only pretended to wake up then, too. And she did snuggle into Brett further, enjoying it all and forgetting that she was parked down the street and was only surreptitiously dating someone else's lover.

She wondered if she could ever get Brett for her own, because she knew she could make Brett happy—for a long, long time. She knew she could do it, and be all that Brett needed.

The phone rang.

Brett pulled away from Victoria to answer it. "Yeah?" she said into the phone.

"Brett," Laura said, "I'm sorry, your first cousin Michael was killed during . . . during . . ." She sounded broken up.

"During a what?" Brett said. She didn't much care for the damsel-in-distress routine. At least not from Laura, or anyone else she loathed and only wanted to see dead.

"A convenience store robbery gone wrong." Her voice went down, as if she was shielding or blocking the phone somehow. Brett wondered where she was calling from. "Apparently he went out late last night to a 7-Eleven to get more beer and . . . and he was killed."

"So another one," Brett said. "Where you at?"

"I . . . I need to get out of here. I wanted to let you know what happened. I need to get home. Mike's wife, Jeanine, called me this morning to let me know and . . . Well, I need to get home before Luke gets suspicious."

"Wait—he doesn't know where you are?" Brett got out of bed to check herself out in the mirror.

"No! I don't need him any more worried about anything. He's got too much going on as it is! This sort of thing isn't good for his health at all." She sounded as if she was putting her foot down. Brett wasn't sure she'd be able to get any more out of Laura now. At least not right at the moment, but maybe later . . .

"Okay, fine. I'll look into this and check with you later," Brett said. She thought she could get away without taking a shower, but all things considered, she didn't think she'd need to. And

Lord only knew, she didn't like ever leaving the house without first showering—and definitely not for something as low priority as one of her family getting killed. "By the way, where did Mike buy it, anyway? I need to know what to ask for and all that to get my hands on the reports and details and such."

"It was the 7-Eleven at Ten and Mound."

"Okay, thanks. I'll be in touch with you later." Brett hung up the phone.

"Who was that?" Victoria asked from the bed, where she lay with the blankets wrapped around her hips, the beautiful olive skin of her torso contrasting against the white sheets and blankets. Her nipples were hard and erect as she stretched.

Brett was sure the stretch was more for her than for Victoria. "That was Laura. Apparently another one of my cousins bought it last night."

"Is that good or bad news?"

"Well, I guess it's kinda good news. First off, there's another one gone, and secondly, with another murder there's likely even more clues lying about for me to find. And this'll be the first time I'll be able to get to a pretty darned recent crime scene with maybe some witnesses and some cops I can talk with."

"So where's the bad, then?"

"Well, I'm supposed to be helping to find the guy who's doing this," Brett said, pulling out shorts, a sports bra, a black T-shirt and socks from her drawers. "And so he's ahead of me by yet one more. Somehow, though, I'm finding it difficult to be very upset at all about it."

"I think I can relate to that."

The phone rang. Brett picked it up again. "Yeah?"

"Brett," Allie said. "Are you going to come and pick me up, or am I supposed to come over there, or what?"

Brett had totally forgotten that Allie had offered to go with her to Luke's church this morning. "Um," she said, looking over at Victoria, whom she'd also asked to go with her. "I'm not sure.

Laura called and told me my cousin Michael was killed last night."

"Oh, God, Brett, I'm sorry," Allie said.

Victoria got up and went into the bathroom.

"I'm not," Brett said into the phone. She looked at the closed bathroom door, trying to decide which woman she should take with her to the church. She didn't want to have to reschedule that appointment, since that would not make a lot of sense, given her cover story and all.

"I don't know what to say," Allie said.

"Anyway," Brett said. "I need to look into that right away, since it's the first murder I'm not coming in cold on." Since Victoria was here, she'd have to come up with an excuse to exclude either from the outing—and then she remembered that she'd told Helen at the church that her name was Victoria Nelson. She'd have a helluva time explaining that to Allie.

'Course, a part of her wanted to tell Allie, since it was because she couldn't trust that Allie would go with her, whereas she knew Victoria would, that she had to use the name she did. She knew it would hurt Allie, and a part of her wanted to hurt her, maybe especially since she felt kinda guilty that Victoria was now back in her bed.

But that wouldn't help her out with Allie in the long run.

"Brett, are you there?" Allie was saying as Brett enjoyed the view of a naked Victoria crawling back into her bed.

"Yeah, I was jotting myself some notes on what I need to do today," Brett said, grabbing the pen and paper from her nightstand to write:

1) *Look up last night's murder*
2) *Get Victoria dressed*
3) *Go to the crime scene*
4) *Go to the church—Helen Anderson, 11 a.m.*
5) *Get police report on last night's murder*

"And since when can't you listen and write at the same time?" Allie said.

"I got woken up by someone I don't like telling me another person I loathe is dead and I'm supposed to do something about it—and now you're all over me about what your priorities and interests are. Y'know, you only want to help when you feel like it, and interfere when you want to, too, although you feel perfectly fine telling me what I should or should not do. It's not fair, Allie!" Brett realized she was sounding like a spoiled kid who needed to be thwapped upside the head and guessed she'd ultimately apologize for this outburst, even though she was right.

"What the hell's gotten into you, Brett? You're the one who's been stalking me, the one who wanted me to help today—"

"And what the hell are you doing calling at this ungodly hour, anyway?"

"I figured your appointment was this morning—"

"You volunteered. And if it's such an imposition, stay home. I'll take care of it myself." Brett slammed the phone down and walked toward the bathroom for a shower, only momentarily stopping to look back at Victoria and say, "So, you gonna join me or what?"

Brett had barely turned on the water and stripped down before Victoria was in the bathroom, wrapping her arms around Brett from behind as Brett adjusted the water.

"Do you like it cool, warm or hot?" she asked Victoria.

"I'd think you of anyone would know I like it hot. The hotter the better."

"Seriously, I don't want to burn you."

"I don't think you can."

"Suit yourself," Brett said, stepping into the shower.

Victoria followed her, allowing Brett to guide her under the spray.

"Turn around," Brett said.

"You sure?"

"Of course." Brett reached up over Victoria's shoulder to grab some shampoo off the rack that hung from the sprayer. She'd rarely shampooed Allie's hair—hell, she'd rarely showered with Allie—and it was apparently obvious to Victoria.

"Get in deep down," Victoria said. "Don't worry about hurting me. Pretend like you're massaging my scalp." She raised her hands to help show Brett what to do. Brett pulled her hands away. "No, no," Victoria said. "I love having my hair washed. Please don't stop." She braced herself against the wall and let Brett wash her hair.

"How am I doing?"

"Better. But I think you'd better wash it again to get the rest."

"Okay, then rinse."

Victoria turned toward Brett and leaned her head back, to rinse the foam out without getting any in her eyes. When she was done, she smiled and twined her arms around Brett's neck, leaning in to kiss her deeply.

Brett reached up, got more shampoo and began working it through Victoria's hair.

Since Brett had told Victoria about the church caper the day before, Victoria had brought appropriate clothes to put on after their shower. Brett couldn't decide if this meant she was prepared or presumptuous; nonetheless, it did make things go quicker and smoother, since they'd go to the 7-Eleven, then the police, and then the church right in a row and it wouldn't take too long since they'd be ready.

Brett looked at her watch. She still couldn't believe Laura had called her at six a.m. Or that Allie called her soon thereafter. She was going to have to have talks with both women about the dire consequences they could experience if they ever even thought of doing so again.

On the bright side, at least this meant they had time to get everything done. Of course, Victoria would be late for work, but Brett had left the box office guy and Frankie messages about it already.

Brett quickly finished dressing, putting on a black suit with a red shirt and red-and-yellow tie. She wanted to make sure the church lady took her seriously and would assume she was a guy. Hopefully Helen Anderson wouldn't be able to tell that it was Brett's voice she had heard on the phone the day before and not Victoria's.

Brett didn't and hadn't taken many showers with Allie, and it had been a long time since the last one. She'd always known she wasn't properly shampooing Allie's hair, but Allie'd never told her how to do it. She'd always loved running her fingers through Allie's long locks, but somehow, along the way, it'd all gotten confused and she'd stopped even trying to doing it so much.

Was it the flush of new, or resumed, love that was making everything with Victoria so nice now?

Brett slipped on her watch, rings and a heavy silver bracelet, then took off the latter, realizing it'd be too much for her purported purpose. But regardless of her costuming to convince the church lady that she was a photographer and fellow reporter, she still put a Beretta on her ankle and her .357 in her shoulder holster, under her jacket, of course.

In the shower, she'd quickly washed herself and her hair while watching as Victoria shaved her legs—but only after Brett had used a fuzzy and some nice shower gel to wash her entire body, paying special attention to her breasts, of course. Brett enjoyed touching Victoria all over like that, and was surprised at how okay she was with Victoria seeing her naked for so long.

While Victoria blew her hair dry and put on her makeup, Brett looked up Michael Higgins on the Web while she also perused several local papers. It didn't take long to find a short article about the hold-up.

Apparently Mikey was on his way out with his beer when the masked man drove up, with his driver waiting for him in the car, blew his head off, then took off.

It almost seemed like a hit, rather than a robbery gone wrong. *Almost* being the operative word. She'd have to prove it to do anything with the information.

"Hello, lover," Victoria said, coming up behind her. "Finding anything interesting?"

"Details on how Mikey bought it."

"Mikey?"

"My cousin. The one who got it last night. Well, early this morning." Brett laid her hands on Victoria's, which were twined about her waist.

"Yeah, I got that. I'm questioning the nickname."

"Michael/Mikey, what's to question?"

"Well, usually the nickname for Michael is Mike, so I'm questioning the familiarity of Mikey."

"Yeah, I remember him."

"And?"

"He deserved what he got. You ready?"

"Yes."

They put on their coats, Brett forgoing the leather in favor of her cashmere trench coat. She figured that although it might be rather upscale, it'd be more to church lady's liking. Anyway, Luke's church *was* in a nice neighborhood—a rather nice neighborhood—so Helen Anderson would likely be quite accustomed to such apparel. She also made sure she grabbed her biggest camera. Her camera phone wouldn't help if she was trying to pass as a photographer.

Brett led Victoria out to the car, locking the house behind her, and they took off.

● ● ●

What Brett didn't see as she and Victoria left her house was that Allie was sitting in a car that was not hers, down around the corner at the end of the street, with a pair of binoculars, watching them walk out together.

She even paid attention as Brett drove Victoria down to her car, and Victoria got in and followed Brett out of the subdivision.

Allie started her car and followed them at a distance. Brett was leading so it was a great deal easier than it might've been, since Brett would be much more aware of any possible followers than Victoria—though Allie had to rethink this presumption when she saw Victoria checking her rearview mirror.

She immediately fell back, remembering that Victoria had helped them recently in a surveillance op and might also have some opportunity to practice such skills when johns followed her home from the theater. Strippers did sometimes get some crazies who were obsessed with them, after all.

She *was* surprised, however—well, almost surprised—that Brett hadn't noticed her. She was sure that her rental car helped, since Brett would likely have noticed her car, or Rowan's, for that matter.

She was just happy she'd been able to get in close enough to the house in the early hours to see how early Brett had woken up and answered the phone. It was almost a fluke that Allie had decided to head out early to check up on Brett.

Allie hadn't been able to sleep, so had gone out to look in on Brett in the early a.m. She didn't think there'd be anything to see, since Brett didn't get up that early. There was actually more of a chance that she'd be still up from the night before than getting up. But still, she hadn't wanted to be home when Rowan woke up, since Rowan'd been making her uneasy of late.

She followed Victoria and Brett to the 7-Eleven at Ten and Mound, and drove on past . . . then kept circling the area, keeping an eye out.

She'd gotten worried when Victoria and Brett both got into

Brett's SUV after talking with people at the 7-Eleven. After all, since they were obviously leaving Victoria's car at the store, she'd have to follow Brett now, who was much more savvy about being followed—plus Victoria was likely to see her as well.

Things were about to get interesting. Thank God most rentals were no longer so clearly labeled as such, due to attacks on tourists in some areas, 'cause then she would've had to borrow a classmate's car, or one from one of Rowan's neighbors.

Chapter Thirteen

Brett adjusted her rearview mirror. "Does that car behind us look familiar?" she asked Victoria.

Victoria turned in her seat to look. "Maybe."

"Thanks for the clarification."

"Why do you ask?"

"It seems familiar. Like maybe it was near my house or something. Then I thought I saw a car like that drive by the 7-Eleven several times when we were in there."

"What did you think about that clerk?" Victoria said, turning back around to look at Brett again instead.

"Well, he wasn't exactly the spiciest taco at the picnic, but look at his job. I mean, he reminds me of a lot of the losers I've hired at the theater."

"What about what he said?" Victoria reached over to run her fingers down Brett's arm.

"What're you doin' there?"

"Just touching you. Should I stop?"

"No." Brett took Victoria's hand in hers. She liked how it felt. "I'm not sure if he'd even realize if someone came in wearing a Bozo the Clown outfit and did a striptease in the center aisle."

"Hey, c'mon, you're selling him short. He did call the police when your cousin was shot."

"I'm surprised he didn't wait until he sobered and straightened up first."

"You think he's a user?" Victoria was running her thumb lightly back and forth across the back of Brett's hand.

"Hell yes." Brett didn't want to do anything to disturb Victoria's hand. It felt too good. She couldn't remember doing these little things with Allie. Or maybe she didn't want to remember. She wondered if she was letting go of Allie and taking Victoria on as a substitute. She wondered if she was in love with the idea of newness. If she'd conveniently forgotten everything that was so good and great about Allie, especially from when they first started dating—both times. Was it all so nice with Victoria because Victoria was trying harder and it was new?

"Yo, Higgins?" Victoria said, reaching over to ruffle Brett's hair, turning even more fully toward Brett. "I asked you a question."

"And I answered it."

"But not about what you thought about what he said."

"Well, the way I see it, you kill somebody and don't take any money off them, it's a hit, pure and simple. Whoever that dude was who shot Mikey, he wasn't there to rob the store, he was out to kill Mikey. I mean, he took off without checking Mikey's pockets and without even bothering to go into the store. I just wonder if any of the surveillance tapes showed anything."

"I'd say we'll never know, except a couple of my regulars are cops, so—"

"I don't like thinking of you with *regulars*."

"Hey, baby, I work for you, and you know I never go beyond lap dances."

"Regardless, it'd be the Warren P.D. who got the tapes."

"And you think nobody from Warren comes down to our neck of the woods. God, Brett, I thought you knew your demographic better."

"We got Warren cops who come in?"

"Hell yes. Besides, if I can't get 'em, I'm sure you can find someone who can. But let me try first."

"Okay. You ready for some breakfast?" Brett asked, turning into a Mickey D's.

"Hell yes."

Brett glanced at her watch. "I think we've got time to eat here, if you'd like."

"Yes, please."

Over breakfast, Brett kept an eye out for the green Dodge Neon she'd seen following them before. Life would've been a lot easier if Detroit wasn't so lousy with American-made cars.

Still, she thought she saw it at least once, maybe twice or thrice . . .

"So what are you thinking?" Victoria said, breaking a corner of her hash brown off with her fingers and putting it in her mouth, just after a bit of her sausage and egg biscuit and just before a sip of coffee.

"Cursing the number of American-made cars in this town. Makes it harder to identify a single one."

"Any identifying stickers or anything?"

"I can't tell. I thought one earlier had a rainbow in the windshield." This made Brett feel much, much better. She thought she'd seen some differences in the car, and now she realized it was a windshield sticker that was in one car. So she *was* simply imagining things. "I can't figure out why anyone would go so far to off Mikey, though." She realized she'd abruptly changed subjects, and was about to explain, but—

137

"The clerk did say he recognized him, so there's a chance that someone was after him and was waiting. Maybe for a couple of nights, but—"

"But especially if someone was working from the inside and could tell the perp when he was leaving the house!"

"So we need to talk to his wife?"

"Got that right. Let's see what Mikey's life was like."

"So if you're thinking someone planned his murder, is there anyone in particular you're thinking of?"

"Not a clue. You ready?" Brett asked, finishing her bacon, egg and cheese biscuit and crumpling up the wrapper.

"Yup."

They both picked up their drinks, threw away their trash, and hit the road again, getting to Luke's church early enough to give it a few drive-bys, with Victoria snapping pics while Brett drove.

"So what is it you're thinking?" Victoria asked, leaning out the window to get another angle. They were figuring no one was paying attention. Still, for other shots, Victoria left the window down and took photos from inside the vehicle.

"That I hate people who talk on the phone while they're driving. God knows people suck enough at driving as it is. Last thing they need is yet another distraction."

"I meant about your brother and this church," Victoria said. "I mean, you obviously think there's something up, otherwise, there's no way you'd be going this far to check it out—especially what with all these photos."

"There's no way my bro's found God and all that shit. No way he's doing charity work or anything like that. This is all a scam. Of that I'm sure. Now, I don't know why Laura's pulled me into this shit, all I can figure is that somebody *is* killing off my family, and that's got her concerned enough she don't think I'm gonna see what little old Lukey is up to with his ministry and all. She's betting the odds, and she's gonna get burned. Bad."

"So you're trying to debunk this ministry right now."

"Yuppers, you got that right." Brett glanced at her watch, then pulled into the lot again and parked. She took the camera from Victoria. "Let's do this."

They walked in, and Brett was immediately impressed with how well Victoria was prepared. She'd written out questions in her notebook and had even acquired a recorder. It seemed to be some sort of a digital model, and Brett noted that she should find out where and when Victoria acquired it, thinking should get one herself. She didn't want Victoria wasting money she didn't have for something to help her, so she could buy it off her, if it was only for this one thing. But then again, Victoria did get it awfully quick, so maybe she'd already had it.

Regardless, she was impressed with how well Victoria played it. Of course, unlike Allie, Victoria had always had to know how to act; after all, life was one big stage for people like Brett and Victoria.

"Excuse me, are you Mrs. Helen Anderson?" Victoria said, walking into the church office.

Brett wanted to slap her, but then she'd have to chop her hand off, since she never wanted to be like her family. But she immediately knew this was so not—

"Why, yes, I am!" the woman said, standing. "You must be that nice reporter I talked with yesterday . . ." She glanced down at her desk, as if looking for the name.

"Victoria Nelson. Yes, ma'am, I am. And I am so happy you could take this time from your busy schedule to meet with me. I hope you don't mind that I brought my photographer along."

Brett held up her camera and smiled.

"Of course not! Oh, dear, if I'd known there were going to be photos, though, I would have taken more time with my hair and makeup this morning!" Helen said, primping.

"You look beautiful," Brett said, snapping a few pictures and keeping her voice low to help with the charade of her being a male. "Smile!"

It turned out Helen *was* a volunteer. Also, she knew nothing of the inner workings of the church—she'd been programmed with the stuff Luke and Laura wanted her to know and repeat to the public. She believed it all, all right, but neither Brett nor Victoria were convinced of anything she said.

And once Helen mentioned that Luke and Laura were coming in that day, Brett signaled Victoria that they had to get out of there, quickly.

But not before getting a tour.

Brett was amazed at how well Victoria knew her, from asking the right questions to getting a full tour of the entire premises, in case Brett later realized that she needed to break in and get more information on the down low.

Before they left, when they were at the front door to the building, Victoria said, "Um, Bob, shouldn't you, er . . . Y'know, before we leave?" When Brett and Helen looked at her blankly, Victoria continued, almost whispering to Helen, "He ate some bad chili last night and, well, you know what I mean, right?"

Brett finally clued in and realized Victoria was setting her up so that she could go and quickly search the church's office, under the guise of using the restroom, while Victoria kept Helen busy with a few last questions in the entryway.

As Brett had already noticed, the filing cabinets all had pretty standard locks, and Helen had obligingly left them all unlocked (with the keys in one of the locks), when she'd come out to greet Victoria and Brett.

Brett had already noted what the keys looked like—one ring with all the filing cabinet keys on it. She was sure it was kept somewhere in the office when not in the locks. That would make things easier if she returned later. For now, though, she quickly ran around the office, using a jacket sleeve to cover her hands to not leave any prints. Granted, she'd left a few prints earlier, quite intentionally, but she wouldn't be able to explain how many she'd be leaving this time. She quickly checked behind all the artwork on the walls until she found a wall safe. She tested the dial and jotted the make and model number in her notebook.

She then went through the filing cabinets. She went through them quickly but methodically. She'd seen which drawer housed the financials Helen had pulled for Victoria, and had, at that point, surmised that all the basic materials needed to apply for grants were kept in there. She was looking for the real dirt, however. So she photocopied anything that looked remotely financial in nature, not believing at all that anything potentially incriminating would be kept here, at the church—unless, of course, Luke and Laura kept such materials at the church in order to ensure plausible deniability if they ever were, in fact, caught.

After all, she didn't think they considered Helen, or any other volunteers who had access to these files, to be any sort of worry as far as being bright and curious enough to work out that there was a scam going on, let alone able to decrypt the financial information to make any sort of sense of it.

She folded up the papers and slipped them into her pockets and roomy camera bag.

Brett finally made her way out of the office, slipping quickly and quietly through the corridors to get to the men's room, slip inside, flush a toilet, wash her hands, then leave the bathroom as noisily as possible.

"Oh, there you are!" Helen said, when Brett walked up to them.

"Helen was about ready to come in after you," Victoria said. That was when Brett realized Victoria had a hand on Helen's forearm. She was sure Victoria'd had to do some fast footwork to ensure Helen indeed did *not* follow her into the restroom to ensure she was okay.

Afterward, while Brett and Victoria walked to the car, Victoria said, "Thank God you came back when you did. She was about to drive me crazy. For God's sake, what were you doing, anyway?"

"A quick search, plus I went into the restroom, in case you guys could hear anything. I don't see why you were so concerned, she didn't seem to want to say good-bye at all. Especially not to you, what with you being so *charming* and *funny*," Brett said, somewhat mimicking Helen.

Brett dropped Victoria off at the 7-Eleven that they'd left her car at, and went on to the Warren Police Department HQ near Common and Van Dyke. Well, actually, off Common between Lorraine and Van Dyke.

It was at the police station that Brett found Allie. "Allie," Brett said, walking up the steps and nodding at Allie, who had stopped on the steps and was apparently waiting for Brett. "What're you doing here?"

"Same thing you are—seeing if I can get a copy of the police report on your cousin's murder."

"You been in yet?"

"Yup. Been and done and no go. It's an open investigation and neither of us is named in it, so we'll have to figure out another way to get your hands on it."

"Okay, then. Thanks for saving me some time." Brett started to turn around, but Allie stopped her.

"You're looking real nice today," Allie said, fondling Brett's lapels.

"I had to play nice with the church lady." Brett reached up to grasp Allie's warm hands before remembering that she was supposed to be pissed off at her. After all, it wouldn't look too good for her to immediately forgive Allie if she didn't want Allie to find out Victoria had gone with her to the church. What was that old saying about what a tangled web we weave, when first we practice to deceive?

"So how'd that go?" Allie asked.

"So-so." Brett turned and began walking away.

"So that's it? You're gonna leave now?"

"Unless you have anything to add, I have a case to work on.

142

One that you wanted me on."

"What's with all this hot and cold, Brett? Last night you were all with the 'love me,' and now you're being an asshole, turning your back on me and running off. I mean, what the fuck? Did you, like, hook up with somebody after we saw each other last night, or what?"

Brett about-faced to get into Allie's face. "You wanna talk about what the fuck? What the fuck were you doing calling just after six in the goddamned morning?"

"We were supposed to meet up to go to the church. You asked me to help last night, remember?"

"You offered to help, remember?"

"Yes, but you wanted my help. So I was calling to set it up."

"Way earlier than necessary and way earlier than I would ever be up. So what made you think to call then?" They were practically dancing around each other on the police department steps.

Allie apparently figured out the dance and planted herself in one spot, attempting to take over the lead. "I wanted to know the plan before I left home."

"You know what? You're all on about—"

"Excuse me, is there a problem?" an officer asked as he walked out of the station.

Brett finally noticed that they'd gotten a bit of an audience—just a few cops, but that was a few too many. "No, no problem, sir," Brett said. She was well aware that she was packing and there was no way this would end well for her unless she walked away now.

Allie was barely in her car before her phone rang. She was pissed off enough that she assumed it was Rowan even before she answered it. "Yes?"

"You were ready to attack me from the first word this morning. Was there any particular reason for that?"

"Oh, no, you can't do that," Allie said, not starting her car. "I was only asking a question."

"What? When?"

"This morning. I called you and asked a question."

"Yes, you did. But I've known you too long, Allie. I can read you like . . . like something I can read well. The latest copy of *Adult Video News*. And this morning you were pissed off from the get-go, and I'm wondering why."

"It was early, I was tired and I was cranky. And now the cops are all watching me, so I'm leaving and saying good-bye. So good-bye."

Brett let it go. For now. And she headed to the office, where she erased the porn-shooting schedule from where the admin assistant had put it on the big whiteboard—God, porn was practically becoming legitimate these days!—and started writing on it.

She went through all her notes to populate the board, writing down who bought it, when they bought it, how it happened and any additional necessary details. She was about to start putting down surnames, but then she realized they would all be "Higgins" since they were all on her father's side, so it'd be kinda redundant.

Who	*When*	*How*
Dad	*12/25 (Xmas)*	*?????*
Cousin Robert	*4/1 (April Fool's)*	*Shot*
Cousin Steve	*5/31 (Memorial Day Holiday)*	*Knifed*
Brother Matthew	*7/4 (Fourth of July Holiday)*	*?????*
Uncle Tim	*9/3 (Labor Day weekend)*	*Car accident*
Uncle Frank	*10/3*	*Stumbled drunk into the middle of I-75*
Brother John	*10/31 (Halloween)*	*?????*
Cousin Mikey	*11/11*	*Shot at 7-11 robbery (Not a robbery????)*

Looking at the list, Brett realized the most amazing thing: That it took seven murders to realize there was perhaps a serial killer on the loose. That was a real statement about her family and what their lives were like.

'Course, there wasn't much of a chance that too many people would put these various means of death together as a serial killer on the loose—even the ones Brett had been able to figure out. Brett herself wasn't certain it *was* a chain of crimes, now that she was looking at it and thinking about it. Before, she'd just jotted her notes on what each person died of—or what she could glean from obituaries and any other Internet articles and/or postings. Serial killers usually kept to one program, one way of killing people. There was nothing to tie these deaths together except that everyone who was dead was related to her and her father.

But, of course, Brett couldn't help but surmise that maybe so many died on or around holidays because the family thing was too much to take. Plus, her family would celebrate any holiday they could think of. She couldn't help but wonder if they'd started celebrating Festivus once *Seinfeld* hit syndication.

She wasn't surprised that no one important—or anyone like a cop or anything—had put together that there was some sort of a serial killer on the loose; her family was involved in so much bad stuff, there was no reason to believe that various others wouldn't be after them. Or that they weren't stupid enough to kill themselves off in a variety of interesting ways.

And Brett couldn't help but think about how uninterested the police were at her mom's house. She wondered how much they disliked her relatives, and how often they were willing to look the other way or not pay attention as far as deaths in her family went.

Especially if they didn't know these Higginses were related to her.

She was sitting back on her desk with a Scotch, staring at the whiteboard and trying to figure out how to determine the missing causes of death, when Frankie came in.

He walked over, poured himself four fingers and propped himself next to her against her desk. "So whatcha doin', boss?"

"Trying to work out how I'm going to figure out how the rest of these folks bought it."

"Maybe this'll help." Frankie handed her a manila folder filled with a bunch of computer printouts, photocopies of handwritten sheets and photos.

Brett flipped through the folder. "Well, that's not right," she said, looking at the photos from when Uncle Tim bought it. From the report and pictures, he'd driven into the side of a building and killed himself late at night.

The problem was that there was an awful lot of blood on the inside of the car. Sprayed across the passenger's side from the driver's side. That didn't look like a car accident to her. It looked more like a shooting.

"So you're seeing it, too, huh?" Frankie said.

"I sure am. And it reminds me of a similar case that happened once upon a time somewhere else—like an ME looked at it, and thought it didn't look much like a drive-by."

"Yup. And the cops that looked into this? Same damned ones you ran into at your mom's house."

"How do you know that?"

Frankie shrugged and downed the rest of his glass. "I talked to them. Let me know if you need me to do anything else," he said as he left.

Brett wondered if the bartender at the bar she'd beaten her nephews down at knew anything. Could be he wore the same blinders the cops did—not seeing anything he didn't want to see, not paying attention when people he figured deserved it got it.

She now went through the folder Frankie'd handed her, carefully reading everything and trying to extrapolate from what she was reading. Fortunately, everyone up until Mikey had gotten it in Detroit, so Frankie'd been able to get quite a bit of information for her.

She then went back over her whiteboard, writing a bit more on it.

Who	*When*	*How*
Dad	*12/25 (Xmas)*	*Got drunk on Xmas, hit head on commode*
Cousin Robert	*4/1 (April Fool's)*	*Drive-by shooting*
Cousin Steve	*5/31 (Memorial Day)*	*Knifed in an alley*
Brother Matthew	*7/4 (Fourth of July)*	*Drink and drug overdose*
Uncle Tim	*9/3 (Labor Day)*	*Car accident @ McNichols and Van Dyke*
Uncle Frank	*10/3*	*Stumbled drunk into the middle of I-75*
Brother John	*10/31 (Halloween)*	*Autoerotic asphyxiation*
Cousin Mikey	*11/11*	*Shot at 7-11 robbery (Not a robbery????)*

Brett savored every word about how her father died, thinking of the irony of him pretty much killing himself trying to take a shit while drunk.

She *didn't* think about everything that happened between her and him in that same john.

She did, however, wish that she'd been his cause of death, that she'd pumped him full of lead. In fact, she wished she had killed every jackass on this list. Every one of them deserved to die, particularly Merry's dad, Uncle Frank. She hated them all with a fiery passion. And though she saw all of this chart as Darwinism in action, she couldn't help but see patterns and how any of these could be murders. Uncle Tim's accident, for instance, could very easily have been someone shooting at him, through his open windows, while he drove, thus causing him to crash.

All much of this would take would be a lack of autopsy, or a shabby one, or lack of a reasonable police investigation. If the cops were like the ones whom she'd met at her mother's, they weren't sad to see her family get what they deserved, which made a lot of sense to her.

Brett could very easily see how any of these deaths could be carefully planned murders. Some of them wouldn't need to be planned at all.

She tried to put it all together in her mind, imagining how it might've all gone down—her father attacked someone in the john on Christmas, whoever it was fought back and he fell over, conking his head on the commode.

That alone made it someone in the family who was responsible.

So why the hell was her family putting her onto it? Did they already know who was responsible? Then why was she being brought in? Why weren't they going after whoever it was themselves?

This suddenly wasn't making sense.

But she decided to stop and think about it all.

The shooting and knifing were obviously deliberate. As was Uncle Tim's murder, although that was more carefully disguised as an accident. Matthew's OD on drugs and booze made sense, but, again, it could be a murder. And someone could've grabbed Frank when he was outta his mind on booze and tossed him out of a car on 75 . . . and made it look like he stumbled out there all on his lonesome. The area he got hit in was bad enough that people often didn't pay too much attention. They put on their blinders of not seeing/not watching/not paying attention.

As for the autoerotic asphyxiation . . . well, she pretty much wanted to jump up and down and applaud that one for its pure brilliance. She loved that he died in the most embarrassing way possible, with a noose around his neck and his trousers around his ankles.

Whoever was responsible was increasing in sophistication. Whoever it was was learning, and fast.

So why was she brought in? What was Luke and Laura's motivation to come to her and make her look at it all?

Did they honestly not realize that if some of these—her father's at least—weren't accidents, then it had to be someone in the family?

Did they want her to be the bad guy? Catch whoever it was so they'd be safe? That might indicate that they already knew who it was, though. So she'd have to grill them enough in the right way and they'd cave and let her know who it was. Then she'd have to decide what to do about it.

'Course, it could be a rival gang, or some folks who wanted to steal some of their business. Or some cops, or the neighborhood watch, wanting to clean up the streets. The rival gang bit didn't make sense, though, since Peter'd said their family wasn't exactly big or important or anything. Just lackeys for others. And if they got killed off, whoever they worked for would just get someone else to do the work.

So cops or neighborhood watch made more sense, except she didn't think there was a neighborhood watch in any of their neighborhoods. They'd need something more like a neighborhood army or militia or something.

Chapter Fourteen

Brett was chowing down on the burger from the Backstage that her and Frankie's new admin assistant, Amber, had brought her for lunch, again appreciating how much such a good woman in such a simple position could do, when her phone rang.

"Uh, yeah, Brett, there's some chick named Tina O'Rourke down here for you," the theater clerk from downstairs said.

"What the fuck does she want?"

"Says she gots some info for you."

"Oh, fuck. Get Amber to walk her up here. I don't need her poking around anywhere she don't belong." Brett continued eating while she heard Amber's phone ring down the hall. She heard Amber go downstairs, then heard the two women come back upstairs.

Part of her thought she should be worried about Tina showing up here, but then again, Tina hadn't shown up here too much, if ever. That she knew of and could remember.

Had Tina ever visited her at her office before?

"So I suppose you're wondering why I'm here," Tina said, coming in behind Amber.

"I told you to wait," Amber said, grabbing her by the shoulder and pushing her back out Brett's door. Brett liked Amber. She had balls. And amazing strength for such a tiny thing. She'd thought about hiring Victoria for the position, but had to be honest that she wasn't at all upset about her and Frankie's choice.

Plus, Amber had nice legs. Excellent ones, in fact.

"Let her in," Brett said, finishing off her burger.

Amber stepped aside to let Tina in, threw Brett a cold look, then left.

Tina walked in and sidled onto Brett's desk, right beside Brett. "So I think maybe I found out some stuff you might want to know."

"Really?" Brett cleaned off her mouth and fingers with her napkin, then threw the trash in the can before leaning back and putting her feet up on her desk. "So tell me about it."

"You know as well as I do that Detroit ain't *CSI*—"

"What the fuck does that mean?"

"The TV show, *CSI*. Detroit cops don't look into things that well. Almost nobody does, in fact."

"Duh."

Tina was getting better at trying to fit in, but her awkwardness in this arena still showed in every word and gesture. "Okay, let's put it this way." She went over to Brett's whiteboard and started erasing things.

"What the fuck do you think you're doing? Nobody plays with my whiteboard but me!" Brett roared, jumping to her feet.

"So are you telling me that receptionist doesn't write on your whiteboard?"

"No, but . . ." Brett was so amazed Tina'd actually said that that she spoke without thinking.

"So here's what I've got and figured." Tina added in lines and marked all the entries *Murder*. She apparently had read it all before she started marking it up. She put in her new entries with another color pen. And, most impressively, she did it all without referring to a single sheet of paper. She obviously knew that Brett would've grabbed any paper out of her hands, so she had to memorize it all.

Who	*When*	*How*
Dad	*12/25 (Xmas)*	*Got drunk on Xmas, hit head on commode*
Bobby Higgins	*2/28*	*Suicide (GSW to head)*
Cousin Robert	*4/1 (April Fool's)*	*Drive-by shooting*
Cousin Steve	*5/31 (Memorial Day)*	*Knifed in an alley*
Brother Matthew	*7/4 (Fourth of July)*	*Drink and drug overdose*
Becky Higgins	*8/15*	*Drowned in empty bathtub*
Uncle Tim	*9/3 (Labor Day)*	*Car accident @ McNichols and Van Dyke*
Uncle Frank	*10/3*	*Stumbled drunk into the middle of I-75*
Brother John	*10/31 (Halloween)*	*Autoerotic asphyxiation*
Cousin Mikey	*11/11*	*Shot at 7-11 robbery (Not a robbery????)*

"So you're saying you found more of my fam that's gotten killed of late?" Brett asked.

"That's exactly what I'm saying. Well, if what *was* on your board was all you knew about." Tina sat with her ass on the arm of Brett's chair and leaned over to take a sip of her soda. "I'm also pointing out that I can be a valuable ally—and can get some info you can't. Also, I know logic can rule us both, so I know you want to follow where the evidence leads. Like *CSI*."

"Hogwash show. Nobody nowhere in the country pays as much attention as they do. And the ex-mayor of Warren, the third largest ciy in Michigan, is now a CSI tech. Shows you a bit of what qualifications are actually necessary."

Tina looked at the board. "Looks to me like somebody, or maybe somebodies, are covering things up." She pulled a compact notebook from her breast pocket. "Here's all I found."

Brett picked up the notebook and flipped through it, seeing that Tina'd hole-punched a lot of pages from the Internet to fit into the small notebook. She'd also written notes to herself. "So why'd you do this?"

"I know you don't have the Warren connections I do. For instance, you probably couldn't get a copy of your cousin Michael's police report. You know, the one from last night. But I got it, and it's in there. I wanted to help you out because I don't think we need to keep busting each other's chops and attacking each other. We can work together well."

"Why do you keep at it, Tina?"

"What do you mean?"

"You keep on trying to make it as if we can work together, even as you harass me and try to piss the hell outta me. You don't know what you want, do you?"

"Yes, I do. But there's no reason to tell you." Tina walked out.

Brett stared after her for a while before again considering the whiteboard. Tina had indeed added in a few Warren murders. Well, deaths. And Brett couldn't help but wonder if there were any others in jurisdictions outside of Detroit.

Regardless, with Tina's new info, if it was indeed accurate, the killer, if there was a killer, had sped up. He'd escalated. He was acting more quickly now. And he was being smart about it—too smart to be a part of her family.

Although Brett wanted to throw all of Tina's info out the door, she decided she ought to at least consider that it might indeed be true. She'd cross-reference the info and see if Tina was leading her on or giving her real intel.

And it was when Brett was thinking about all of this that her phone rang.

"Omigod, Brett," Laura said as soon as Brett answered. "I don't know what to do!"

"What's going on?"

"Marie, your cousin, Marie, has been kidnapped."

"What the fuck are you talking about?" Brett was so startled that she stood up to yell down into the receiver.

"We haven't seen Marie in more than twenty-four hours, and then we received a ransom note. What I'm talking about is kidnapping."

"Are you saying that you've seen Marie lately?"

"Yes. She lives with us and volunteers at the church. We see her every day, and that's why I know she's missing and there's something not right about it—she didn't come back here last night after working at the food bank!"

"How was she doing?"

"Marie?"

"No, Zippy the Wonder Toad. Of course I'm talking about Merry—Marie!"

"Were you close to her, Brett?"

"Like hell you don't know!"

"I don't. Remember, I didn't know you when you were growing up. I don't even know you now."

Brett wished she could see Laura right now, because people often gave a lot of physical clues when they were lying. Granted, from what she'd read, Brett was of a mind to think that psychopaths didn't give out the usual signs of lying, since they didn't seem to have any sense of right or wrong, so had no problems with deception.

And, from what she knew, Brett had no idea whether Laura was a bona fide psychopath. But still, she wished that she could see Laura, just for a chance to see if she was lying or not, because she was sure Laura had to be lying. Brett was sure Merry had died years ago, yet she couldn't help but get excited that perhaps Merry was indeed still alive and she could perhaps see her again.

"So why are you contacting me with this?" Brett said.

"Because you're the only person I know who can come up with the money they're asking for!"

"So you're admitting that you're coming to me for money—you, wife of a rich evangelist type?"

"We're not rich! I've told you that!"

"Yes, but I don't buy it."

"Okay, fine, Brett. I don't care what you believe. You're the person in the best position to look into this. You're already looking into the murders—"

"Why do you keep saying they're murders?" Brett asked, looking at her whiteboard. "Most of 'em look for all the world like accidents."

"Okay, fine. I only told you about your dad and brothers. Two of your cousins, before Michael, were also killed—one with a knife and the other during a drive-by shooting. Those were the two who made me think there was a killer on the loose. Plus, well, John wasn't the sort that would know how to tie a proper knot for hanging."

"So who all do you know about?"

"Your father, brothers, and cousins Robert, Steve and Michael."

"Is that all?"

"Your uncles Frank and Tim, too."

"And you didn't feel like telling me all this because . . . ? You didn't think more murders were relevant?"

"I know you had it bad growing up and I didn't want to mention anyone else who might've . . . made things bad for you."

"You didn't think I'd . . . I dunno, maybe figure out there were more guys who got it?"

"I assumed you would. Now I know you are as good as the

papers made you out to be."

"It's not like you're paying me, or having me audition for the part of the one who might save your asses—*all* of your asses. And unless you stop withholding information and tell me everything you know, right now, I'm gonna walk away from it all."

"So what do you want from me?"

What Brett *wanted* was information on Merry, but she couldn't trust Laura to tell the truth on that. Especially not if Laura was looking to get money out of Brett. So instead she said, "Tell me who all you know who's died so far. And everything you know about all the murders. Or accidents. Whatever the hell they are." She walked over and started writing even more notes on her whiteboard.

Laura sighed. "I've got some newspaper clippings, and I know quite a bit about some of the others. Why don't you come over? I can make us a bite to eat, we can discuss it all, and you can look around to see if you can find any clues about your cousin Marie's kidnapping. Maybe there's something in her room, or—"

Brett stared at the board. She should investigate Luke and Laura's house and talk with *both* of them. Plus, she did want to . . . see Merry's things. And she hoped Merry was still alive—hoped it enough, in fact, to be tempted to look into this, if only on the off chance Laura *was* telling the truth and Merry was still alive and had been kidnapped.

If Merry had been kidnapped, Brett was willing to do almost anything to get her back and keep her alive. She glanced at her watch. "Fine, I'll be there at four."

Brett was glad she'd stayed dressed in her suit from this morning. Looking this damned good felt like she was wearing a set of armor.

She took a picture of her whiteboard with her camera phone, then sat and wrote down everything that was on the board in her notebook and had Amber make copies of it while she e-mailed Allie and Victoria the picture of her whiteboard—separately, of course—asking each to look it over and tell her if they saw anything she was missing, or had any ideas.

She did copy and paste the message to send them both the same one, though.

She made sure both her guns were ready to go, then she grabbed pepper spray and a knife from her desk and put those in her pockets.

She wanted to be ready today. If part of her shut down, she wanted to have other ways to act than shooting someone.

But she vowed that if anyone tried anything, she'd be ready to kill.

Focusing on that kept her mind away from all the bad stuff—like thinking her Merry might possibly be alive. Even having that hope was too much, and she knew she could be crushed too easily with it.

If she was truly going to PI this case, she needed to go to Luke and Laura's, talk to them and examine the premises. She made sure her camera was ready to go again, then went down to the dancers' dressing room.

"Hey babe," she said to Victoria when she walked in.

"Hey, honey," Victoria said. Cybill and Heather were sitting near her. The three appeared to be painting each other's toenails.

Brett looked at Victoria and pointed upstairs. Victoria hobbled up the stairs after her with cotton balls between her toes.

"Hey, honey, nice to see you again," Victoria said to Brett, wrapping her arms around Brett's neck and kissing her.

"I e-mailed you a picture of my clues list," Brett said when they pulled away from each other. "And here's a handwritten copy of everything I've got. I'm going to meet with my brother and his wife. While I'm gone, I'd like you to look this over and see if there's anything I'm missing."

Victoria, who looked a little miffed at how abruptly Brett had pulled away, now said, "Do you want me to go with you?"

"No. I'm ready this time."

"You might be armed, but are you ready?"

"Yes, I am. Laura told me my cousin's been kidnapped."

"And why do you care?"

"It's my cousin Merry."

"The only one in your family you give a damn about."

"Got it in one."

"I can go with you and stay in your car, in case anything happens."

"No."

"Well, feel free to call me if you want me to come."

"Thanks. But really, let me know if I'm missing anything."

"Will do."

Luke and Laura's house did not look like the house of people who were barely eking out a living. It looked more like a showplace home, the home of folks who didn't have to wonder when or where their next steak was coming from.

Brett pulled out her phone and took a few pics of the front of the house, then walked around it, snapping more photos. She noticed exactly when Laura noticed her, and continued along on her picture-taking way. She'd driven by before and snapped a few pics, but now she could do so to her heart's content. So she did.

She continued circling the house and photographing it, feeling almost as if someone was watching her, which was easily explainable when Laura came outside and said, "What are you doing?"

"Investigating the scene. Outside in and all that. You don't mind, do you?"

"No, of course not." Still, Laura followed Brett.

"Good, 'cause if you did, it would make me think you were trying to hide something."

Laura pointed to a window. "That's Marie's room. In case you want to, I don't know, look for fingerprints in the grass or any-thing."

Brett stopped. She turned. She stared at Laura.

"What? I don't know what you're looking for or anything—only that you're looking for clues or something!"

"You don't actually think I could fingerprint the grass, do you?" Brett wasn't sure if Laura was testing her, having her on, or was merely that stupid.

"I don't know. I'm not a PI or anything. I'm a nurse." She stayed right by Brett as Brett examined Marie's window, down to taking photos of the grass in the area—in case there were any footprints—and running her fingers along the window ledge.

"People who think you can fingerprint the grass are wreaking havoc on the criminal justice system," Brett said, doing a chinup, her fingers tight on the windowsill. She held herself up with one arm and tried to open the window. It was locked. She peered into the room. The drapes were closed.

"What do you mean?" Laura said while Brett snapped photos of her backyard garden.

"Fact: In Washtenaw County—y'know, where Ann Arbor is—someone on a jury noted the cops hadn't bothered to finger-print the lawn." Brett turned and looked at Laura, who looked as if she was waiting for the punch line. "You can't fingerprint a goddamn lawn!"

"Please, Brett, we don't like to use the Lord's name in vain around here. Also, we don't know as much about detective work as you do."

"Laura, I ain't no detective. I do, however, know how to read. And you came asking me for help, so if you're gonna try to give me rules and crap, you can go—"

"You're right. I'm sorry. Please, help us get Marie back."

No male in Brett's lineage ever asked for forgiveness. They never said, *I'm sorry.* Never. And she couldn't imagine any of their wives doing so, either.

Yet Laura had.

Interesting.

Brett turned to Laura. "Tell me this: Why should I believe for one instant that some serial killer suddenly decided to dive into kidnapping?"

"I have no idea. There's no reason for it, but Merry's missing, and we received a ransom note! I can only think to blame myself, since the only thing that's changed—the only reason for this killer to suddenly go into kidnapping—is because of *you*! And I was the one who brought you in!"

"What the fuck you talking about?"

"Something must have happened to make the killer take Marie. The only thing that's changed is that I begged you to help us, and you did! The killer must have realized you were helping us and that you have money and maybe you'd pay for her. It doesn't make any sense, but that's the only thing I can think of to explain this."

"So you're saying this is all my fault?"

"Brett . . . can you tell me . . . do you have a connection with Marie? I mean, first you were talking about her with your mother, right?"

"Yes . . ." Brett was beginning to feel cornered, just like in the old days. She didn't like the feeling one bit.

"If whoever's killing everybody figured that out—"

"How the hell would they?" Brett asked, trying to regain control of the situation.

"If you really had such a good and *special* relationship with her, any of your family might know, and I was already realizing it because I'd heard you talk about it with your mother, in front of several other members of your family."

"Murderers don't go into kidnapping."

"And they always kill in the same way."

"That's an urban legend. It's the things about their crimes that satisfy them that don't change, but sometimes they change

160

their crimes up to confuse the police or make it more difficult to track them down or implicate them." Brett spoke almost without thought, since she was quite focused on Merry and her disappearance. She already knew she was overlooking the obvious, but it was so personal to her, she couldn't help it.

"You've been doing your homework, then," Laura said.

"I would, if I needed to. But I didn't need to since I already knew such basic info. Since I'm always surrounded by criminal types, I find it smart to learn more about them. And I'd think you'd know that much, too, if you were working in rehab when you met Luke."

"Well, yes. I did. That's the only reason I'd believe this entire kidnapping thing for one instant. But the facts are that Marie's gone, we've got a ransom note, and it looks like there's a killer on the loose. Those could be unrelated, but it seems more likely that it's not."

Brett didn't like all these admissions Laura was making one bit. It was making her even more sure she was being set up. But she didn't want to bet Merry's life on it. "Let's go inside," she eventually said, still staring at Laura. She'd already looked up the house online—to figure out where Luke and Laura lived, as well as how much they'd bought the house for and what it was currently estimated at. Through the hard years of her life, she'd discovered information and learning could be power.

Laura led them back to the front door. It had two deadbolts in addition to the regular lock. And the door was a steel job, a nice, solid number. From what Brett had seen from the outside, the house looked secure, with all doors having multiple locks. No bars on any windows, but now that she was inside, she could see the alarm system.

"When do you turn that on?" Brett said, pointing out the alarm.

"At night, whenever we're not at home. And it's got different levels, so we turn it on when we're home for the night, too."

"What's the password?"

"Uh, um . . . why should I share that with you?"

"You've asked me for my help, and I need to know that in order to determine how secure this house is. I'm not apt to believe anything you say—about Merry—Marie—being kidnapped or anything else. Also, given our collective histories, *I'm* the most reliable one of all of us. Plus, I'm the one who can easily walk away from you and this house and this entire goddamned situation."

"It's nine-nine-nine."

"Nine-nine-nine?" Brett asked, examining the unit and jotting down the make, model and serial number in her notebook. She also took a picture of it, as well as of the front door and all its locks.

"It's six-six-six turned upside down."

"Huh." Brett looked around. "This doesn't look like the home of people who are dirt poor." She wandered freely throughout the main living area, noting that there were indeed wheelchair ramps and other amenities that made the dwelling fully accessible.

She also noticed the 60-inch plasma TV, full home theater system, gourmet kitchen—

"We often have to entertain major funders and important people from the church. We wouldn't live like this if we didn't need to."

"Yeah, and let me guess—those major funder types often come over to watch the big game on your big TV."

"Your brother is not a well man. Some days he can't do too much, and watching TV is one of his few solaces."

"Yeah, right." Brett realized the mudroom door was unlocked. "Do you usually leave this door unlocked?"

"Well, yeah. Yes. We always keep the garage door closed."

"Except when you're coming or going or carrying in the groceries, preheating the car or some other things, I'd suppose."

162

"Well, yes, I'd guess you're right . . . But we don't leave it open if we're not here and watching it."

"Yup, that's about what they all say." Brett walked around the Range Rover to the back of the garage. The door was unlocked. "And do you keep the back door of the garage closed?"

"We never unlock that!"

"Well, it's unlocked now. Something that could've been done by anyone who was in the garage at any time. And, for the record, opening a garage door ain't rocket science. But still, you make it mighty easy for someone to hide in the garage and slip right into the house when you're not looking—if they don't do it while you're back at the car." She took pics of the Rover and the entire garage, including all the power tools located out there, tools that included a hedge trimmer, weed whacker, woodworking tools . . .

"So are you saying that whoever grabbed Merry got in through the garage?" Laura said.

Brett picked up a pen from the workbench and weighed it roughly in her hands. It was nice. "Yes." She used the pen to draw a rough sketch of the garage in her notebook and add in some other notes. She tried not to react to anything Laura said, because everything about all of this stunk worse than a toxic chemical dumping site.

She walked around the Rover, looking for anything out of place or wrong with the vehicle, taking pictures of any dents, paint scrapes and other markings. She even examined the wheels, looking for wear and dirt.

When they walked back in, Brett took careful note of the leather and fur coats hanging in the mudroom.

"Luke didn't—hasn't—said much about you," Laura said, following Brett. "He's said enough about his previous life and family and all that for me to . . . guess."

Brett ran a finger along a shelf. Lots of books, no dust. But when she picked up a hardcover book and opened it, she could

163

tell it was the first time the book had ever been opened. "You have a maid, you buy things—like these books—that you never use, open or read."

"We have to try to maintain a particular image. Can I get you anything to drink?"

"Keeping up with the Bradys, huh?" Brett said, ignoring the offer of a beverage.

"We could live on the streets, wearing rags, but you only give a dollar to a homeless person."

"I don't give 'em anything."

"And that's what I mean—people give money to people who've got it. We live well enough so important people will want to come and visit us. We dress to fit in with them—or maybe just below them, just a hair below them, so they can feel above us, but not uncomfortably so. And we do all this to raise money to help the less fortunate. And are you sure? We've got iced tea, lemonade . . . or maybe you'd prefer a cocktail?"

"I also know that a lot of those street paupers make more in a day than I do. Else they're criminals or dopeheads."

"Then you could offer them food instead of money." Laura pulled a plate of little sandwiches out of the fridge and another plate with shrimp and what looked like maybe crab or seafood cakes out of the oven.

Brett wondered who had made all the goodies, but she ignored them and continued through the house, taking pictures. "Yeah, I've done that a few times. Mostly the burgers get thrown back in my face, so I don't do that anymore." She felt as if she was casing the joint and, in a way, she was, because she wouldn't have a problem breaking into the place if she needed to. She'd just have to wonder if Laura'd been telling the truth about the security code. She'd have to try it out before she left. It would be one nice way to check the veracity of what Laura said.

Because she sure as hell wasn't going to take anything these dirtbags said at face value. Too many people apparently did that already, but she, at least, knew what they were made of—shit, pure and simple.

And Lord knew, the pictures of her brother in a wheelchair with a blanket over his legs, making as if to help kids or homilize to poor people or feed folks at a soup kitchen, made her want to throw up.

'Course, she also wanted to see his legs without the blanket, since he always made sure they were totally covered, so no one could tell what they looked like—how strong or weak or skeletonized they were.

So far she'd seen nothing to prove to her that her brother was as bad off as Laura said he was; she did, however, see that he lived a spoiled rich life and was quite enamored of himself, given the number of pictures of him that there were around. There was even a wall of newspaper clippings that featured him. And some even included Laura.

Two included Merry. In the photos and articles.

"Take me to her room," Brett said. *Into the belly of the beast*, she thought to herself.

Chapter Fifteen

Luke and Laura's room was on the main floor, which made total sense if Luke was wheelchair-bound. Laura tried to stop Brett, but still, Brett went into the room and checked out the bathroom, complete with its full-size Jacuzzi.

"It's incredibly therapeutic for Luke," Laura said.

"Yeah. I'm sure he needs to relax after all that hard talking he's always doing."

"Your brother's a changed man, whether you want to believe it or not, Brett."

"Changed into what?"

"He's a good man, now, Brett."

"I'd much prefer him as a dead man, myself. Speaking of—if he's so concerned about Marie, where is he now?"

"He didn't think you'd want to see him. Or that you were ready to. This is her room," Laura said, stepping aside and letting

Brett walk into the supposed room of Marie.

"So where is he now?"

"Talking with a few friends in the police department. It's entirely unofficial, since we were told not to contact the police, but he figured it wouldn't hurt."

Everything in the room was neat and orderly, entirely unlike how Merry ever was. "So these supposed cop friends couldn't help with the entire serial murderer issue?"

"Nothing has happened around here, so they couldn't help out much. They did what they could, but ultimately we thought you might be a better resource and help with it than they would be."

"Yeah, whatever," Brett said, running her fingers over the books in this room. They'd obviously been read, including all of the Harry Potter books, *The Lion, the Witch and the Wardrobe*, all of the Chronicles of Prydain by Lloyd Alexander, and the Boxcar Children, all of which Brett remembered Merry loving when she was younger, except, of course, for the Harry Potter books.

When she was younger—much, *much* younger. Parts of the room were like some frozen-in-time museum, while others were perfectly normal and up-to-date. Brett went to the bed and sniffed the blankets and pillow, which held reminiscences of what Merry smelled like years ago. Brett wasn't sure if it was the last perfume she'd smelled on Merry or what—because Merry hadn't worn perfume when she was younger, so Brett didn't know how Luke and Laura could replicate Merry's smell if Merry hadn't actually lived with them. Of course, little-girl smell and Merry's soap and shampoo would've been close to what she would've smelled like, wouldn't it? Have a little girl stay over in this room for a while, using Merry's old products, and the deceit might work.

But the fact that all the books were newish—like, bought in the last decade—made sense, since Merry wouldn't've had the ones from when she was a child. Anything her family hadn't destroyed, she'd lost when she moved, or sold when she became a drug-addled stripper.

Brett opened the closet and glanced through that, but she couldn't bear to go through the drawers, not yet at least, since that would feel too much like invading Merry's space, and she didn't want to go searching through Merry's underthings, not now, not when there was a chance they might actually *be* Merry's underthings, and . . .

. . . and Brett stopped the memories from coming and overwhelming her again. She didn't want that to happen here, now. Not in front of Laura.

So instead she went to the computer and moved the mouse to wake it up. It didn't, so she looked down and saw that it was turned off. She turned it on again.

"I don't know her password or anything," Laura said.

"Don't look like she's got one," Brett said. "In fact, it doesn't look like she's used this much at all."

"We only just got it for her."

"Huh. Like, yesterday?" It didn't seem as if there was much on the PC.

"Did you try looking under recent documents or anything like that?"

Brett opened Word and did that, finding Merry's diary. She couldn't bear to look at it, at least not in front of Laura. "Looks like she's got a journal or something on this. Do you mind if I take it home with me?" She shut down the system.

"Can't you e-mail what you need to yourself?"

Brett had already thought about doing that, but she didn't know how to do it without being obvious. Plus, she kinda wanted the entire box so she could thoroughly search it. Then she remembered who she was, so she reached down to unplug the machine. Maybe she could talk Leisa into taking a look at it.

"What're you doing?" Laura asked.

"I'm taking the computer."

"I'm sorry, I can't let you do that," Laura said, moving as if to stop Brett.

"If you want me to help you, then I'm taking it with me."

"What if the police want it?"

"You said you're not involving them."

"But we might!"

"So you don't need me," Brett said, stepping away from the computer with her hands in the air.

"No! That's not what I'm saying at all!"

"Your choice—me or it. You can't have both. I either take it with me, or walk away without it and never speak with you again."

"I . . . I don't know what to do. Can we wait for Luke?"

"No. Because that tells me you're lying. Good luck and good riddance," Brett said, walking out of the bedroom.

"Wait—fine, take it with you!"

"Too late. I'm outta here." Brett had been on the edge of her temper since hearing that Merry was kidnapped. It had only gotten worse as she heard more from Laura—more of what she was sure were lies and parts of some sort of a setup—and then that she was responsible for Merry being kidnapped. She was now closer than ever to the breaking point.

"Brett! Can you leave your family like this?" Laura ran to keep up with her, clutching at her.

Brett whipped around and caught Laura by the wrist of the hand that held her. She quickly flipped Laura around and held her against the wall with her hand twisted up behind her. "Don't ever grab me like that again, understand?"

"Yes," Laura said. It sounded as if she might be scared or in pain. Brett didn't believe that, so she twisted Laura's arm a bit more, until Laura acked in response.

Brett held Laura's arm up behind her back, pushing Laura face first into the wall. She whispered in her ear, "If you're playing me, you're going to pay for it—both you and your hubby.

Next time I won't just walk away, you'll have to pay for it—the time you've cost me, and all the pain and suffering you've cost me as well. Remember, I hate you and your hubby and his entire family as well. I'd just as soon see all of you dead. So stop fucking with me." She twisted the arm a bit higher, now moving it so that she was sure Laura was in pain.

"Yes, yes."

"And don't ever, *ever*, pretend to be in pain when you're not. 'Cause then I'll make sure you are, got it?" Brett said, pushing the arm a bit higher. She wasn't pleased that Laura'd been trying to play her. Actually, it pissed her off, and right now was so not the time to be pissing her off, 'cause she was so pissed off in general, she'd so like to cause pain to some people who deserved it that she was considering going out on a vigilante spree.

It was so nice to split the heads of folks who deserved to have their skulls cracked.

"So you still want me on the case?" Brett asked.

"Yes."

"So I can go back and grab that computer and anything else I want from Merry's room?" Brett ratcheted her arm a bit farther.

"Yes." Laura no longer even tried to struggle. Brett could only guess that she was afraid struggling would hurt even more.

"Good." Brett released her arm, then grabbed her by her shoulders and shoved her against the wall. "'Cause right now I'm thinking y'all are trying to play me, and I don't like that one bit. In fact, it's pissing me off, and you wouldn't like me when I'm well and truly pissed off."

"I believe you." Laura was barely whimpering now.

"Good. 'Cause you gotta know that I won't be happy or pleased if I find out that you're ever lying to me about anything ever again."

Laura stared up at her.

"This is where you're supposed to say, 'Got it.'"

"Got it."

170

"Now mean it."

"Got it."

"I still don't believe you."

"I've got it, damnit, I've got it, Brett!" Laura was crying and looked about ready to drop to her knees.

"I finally believe you." She released Laura, then looked right into her eyes, with one arm against the wall on either side of her. "Now realize that I'm about ready to kill you or have you killed if you keep up with this shit. If you're lying to me, realize the only way it'll end is with *you dying*."

Brett went back to Merry's supposed bedroom, grabbed the PC, threw a bunch of books and other items into a backpack sitting there, and left, walking right by Laura, who was sitting on the floor, crying.

Brett still didn't believe her. "By the way, glad to see you never break your no-swearing rule," she said as she grabbed a nice cloth napkin in the kitchen, filled it with some of the little sandwiches and cakes, and left.

And since she now had a full family tree on the Higgins side of the derangement, she drove by the houses/apartments/street corners of all her living relatives that she could track on her way home.

She wanted to do some damage to someone because she was in a violent mood. And her family were the ones who most needed brutalizing that she could think of. So she stalked them all, looking for someone to beat the living hell out of.

But she couldn't find any that needed any immediate brutalizing. Plus, she knew she was getting totally paranoid now, but she felt like someone was watching her—and the first rule of doing anything illegal or that can get you locked up is to do it in front of witnesses. So she took pics and tried to take her mind off Merry, but she did about kick herself when she realized she hadn't gotten a copy of the ransom note, so would have to return to Luke and Laura's.

She felt like a goddamned idiot.

And she didn't want to turn around, because she was certain Luke would be there, and she didn't want to see him. Not now. Not ever again.

So she went home, carried everything in, then took care of a hit, bombed a few drug fronts, called in a back-up squad and took over another family's warehouse, and brutalized some shop-keepers into cutting her in for a bit of the action on her Godfather game on the Wii. It was proving quite helpful with any anger management issues she might have.

Plus, it was damned fun!

She thought about ordering a pizza but remembered the napkin o' goodies. She'd thought about feeding the sandwiches and cakes to a neighbor's dog—or maybe a raccoon or squirrel—but was kinda hungry. She sniffed them, thinking that it'd be ridiculously obvious for Luke and Laura to drug the food. The best they could do then would be to tie her up and torture her or something, but they'd have to know her business partner would likely notice her missing and come to kill them.

So she ate the food and continued playing the game until the doorbell rang.

"Hey, baby," Victoria said as soon as Brett opened the door. "I haven't heard from you, so I decided to check in on you between shows." She stepped inside and held up a bag. "And I brought dinner."

"Oh. Thanks." Brett walked into the living room to shut off the game, but first she played it to the next available save.

"You're addicted to that, aren't you?" Victoria said, wrapping her arms around Brett from behind, letting Brett play to the save before she set out the plates and pulled some drinks from the fridge.

"Some might say it's better than smashing in the faces of some johns when I get pissed off," Brett said. "What'd you get?"

"I brought us some chicken Caesar salads. Don't make that

face. You don't eat enough veggies and you know it. You've got cheesy garlic bread, too, though."

Brett eagerly ripped open the foil-wrapped package Victoria indicated.

Victoria reached across the table to run a hand along Brett's cheek. "You can be such a kid sometimes, Brett."

"Why? 'Cause I like cheesy garlic bread?"

"I wasn't complaining."

"So, um, you got one more show to do tonight, right?" Brett asked.

"Yes, why?"

Brett pulled out her phone and called the theater. "Yeah, Tom? This is Brett. I need Victoria to help me out with a special project, so she won't be in for the last show tonight. Can you see if some other girl can cover for her? You can waive the stage fee, since it's a one-show-only deal." She continued eating, while Tom flipped through to suggest some girls to her. "Listen, I don't need details or diagrams. Just take care of it for me." She hung up.

"What do you need me for?"

"I forgot to get a copy of the ransom note, so we need to go back to my brother's."

"Didn't want to do it by yourself?"

"Hell no!"

Victoria sat back with her fingers steepled in front of her mouth. "Tell me, Brett, with all your PIing about recently, have you gotten anything to, say, bug a house or trail a car with?"

"What are you thinking?"

"Well . . . I looked over that list you gave me and my first thought was that your family seems as fatally stupid as mine. Also that the deaths could be accidents, unrelated or related."

"Yeah, well I already knew all that. I was looking for anything I might've overlooked. Y'know—the not-so-obvious stuff."

"Well, yeah, but if you're thinking what I'm thinking, then

you're probably wondering what the real reason they pulled you in on this is."

"Yeah, sure, fine, I was."

"What better way to find out than to hear them? And maybe you can find out what's up with your brother Luke at the same time, too."

"What the hell are you talking about, Victoria?"

"I'm saying we bug their place." Victoria shrugged and finished off her salad.

Brett stared across the table. She knew it'd be illegal if she were to bug her brother's house, but she was sure her brother was a grade-A fraud, which was also illegal. She looked across at Victoria. "I like how you think. And I don't have what we need, but I think I know where to get it all."

They finished eating and Victoria cleaned up while Brett went online, finding a couple of spy shops in the area. "I think I've found a place with everything we'll need."

Chapter Sixteen

Allie watched when Brett went from the theater up to her brother's house. She was thankful she'd looked through all the information she'd accumulated—all the information about all the crimes and players she could find—and so kinda figured where Brett was heading, which was a good thing since she'd lost her en route.

Even though Allie'd been professionally trained on how to follow people and had used the skill a lot through the years, what with first being a detective and then working with Brett on a variety of escapades, she'd had some tough times throughout the day. Even the beginning, when Brett and Victoria'd been really dodgy when they'd showed up at Luke's church, the Ministry of the Healing Hand, had been difficult. They'd driven around and through the parking lot and the surrounding neighborhood quite a bit before even going in.

It'd been tough, but Allie'd managed to creep up next to the building and peer in through the windows to watch Victoria, Brett and the church lady, then Victoria and the church lady.

She couldn't believe Victoria had spent the night with Brett—it was especially mind-boggling since last night Brett had been trying to woo her back, trying to get Allie back again.

And then Brett had gone home and spent the night with Victoria, in the bed she shared with Allie—and now she had Victoria playing the part Allie was supposed to play! She was working a case with Victoria, when she'd gotten involved because of Allie!

Now Allie dodged around until she saw Brett going through the office, searching and photocopying, before returning to Victoria and the church lady. Allie knew it was risky, but she needed to hear something, anything—perhaps a name, either the name of the church woman or the name she called Victoria—so she sneaked over to the door and tried to listen while Victoria and Brett left.

When she didn't get that, when she couldn't hear anything, she ran back to her car, getting there seconds before Brett and Victoria got to theirs.

She was glad she'd had the foresight to rent this car the day before. At the time, she'd had a bit of a thought that maybe she and Brett would use the extra vehicle to help them follow whomever they needed to.

Well, she'd also figured she might end up following Brett herself to see how much of what she said was true—because she was very close to believing Brett and taking her back.

Looked like that wouldn't be happening anytime soon.

"Yes, ma'am," Allie said after dialing the Ministry of the Healing Hand. "I'm from the *Roanoke Record* and I'm looking for one of our reporters that I think had an earlier appointment with you—"

"Oh, that nice Victoria Nelson. I'm sorry, but you just missed her. She just left."

"Oh, well, thanks anyway."

She loved Brett and wanted her back, but she couldn't keep letting Brett use her. She remembered how pissed off she'd been when she'd realized, so many years ago, when she was with Brett the first time around, that Brett had been cheating on her with Storm.

At that time, that was enough to get Allie to dump Brett. It was five years before Allie'd even spoken with Brett again— enough time to make Brett go to the dark side and for Allie to get through college and the police academy and become a cop. Allie'd been pulled in by Randi to help try to catch Brett at all the wrongdoing she did.

They'd been through a lot since that time—what with Allie thinking she'd killed Brett, Brett faking her death and running away with Allie . . . At the time, Allie thought it meant something that Brett had forgiven her for all but killing her. She thought that maybe they'd gotten over Brett's cheating on her and that Brett could be monogamous with her.

She'd wanted and needed to believe it enough that she'd ignored any signs that Brett was cheating on her, and every time Brett did something extraordinary to help Allie or her friends, like jumping off a building after Randi, it was a sign that Brett loved her and was faithful to her.

And now Allie heard the name of the woman whom Brett had always planned on taking with her to the church this morning, and even as she realized that when Brett asked her, Allie, to go with her when she knew she'd intended Victoria to go with her—because Brett had obviously given the woman at the church Victoria's name—Allie couldn't help but think about how wrecked Brett had been when they'd moved to Alma, Michigan, and couldn't help but wonder if it'd been because of the ghost, or if she'd been having an affair with one or two ghosts. She remembered everything that happened when Brett worked at

177

that ad agency in Lansing and wondered if Brett had indeed been having an affair with Sara, her boss there. Or if she'd ever scored with that cheerleader later on—or with any of her dancers.

Allie felt like a complete idiot. She'd ignored so very much all these years, and now she realized Brett might've been cheating on her with dozens of women. She couldn't help but think about the women in her women's studies classes who talked about overcoming victimization and all that shit. She'd hated how her fellow students had talked about their relative powerlessness—she didn't like the feeling that evoked in her, but she didn't have enough fingers and toes to count all the women she knew about or had heard of who were victims.

Even her own mother had been a victim, killed by Kirsten, one of Allie's exes, the same ex who killed her father and then, later, almost killed Brett and her. The one Allie'd killed when she thought she'd killed Brett.

Allie *really* didn't like being a victim, and all those women in her class seemed to dwell on being victimized and she didn't want to even think about it. Allie'd been a victim enough in her past and never wanted to think about it again, let alone experience it.

And now Brett had again made her a victim.

And she wasn't happy about it. So she felt increasingly justified as she thought about all of this as she followed while Brett dropped Victoria off at her car. She fell back even farther once Brett took off in one direction and Victoria took off in another—probably toward the theater to go to work. Allie needed to give her more space now since Brett wouldn't be talking with Victoria while driving anymore, making her much more likely to notice if someone was following her.

But Allie knew Brett and knew her well, so she knew how to follow her now—and knew the sweet trick of figuring out where Brett was headed ahead of time—where else could she be headed in that neighborhood?—and getting there ahead of Brett so she could look as if she was leaving when Brett was entering.

No matter that she lied to Brett about not being able to get the Warren police report about her cousin Michael's death. She knew neither of them would be able to get it, and she knew what she said was true, so it made perfect sense for her to use her knowledge to get a step ahead of Brett and make it look as if she *wasn't* following Brett.

It was a really cool and sweet move and Allie was particularly proud of it. She was sure even Brett would've been impressed with that bit of improv—after she got done being furious about it.

It'd been difficult, but at the police station, as she talked with Brett, she kept it in mind that the last Brett knew of, Allie'd been flirting with her and been all right with the idea of helping her. Of course, that morning, Brett hadn't exactly been nice to her, and Brett had woken up with Victoria, but at that time, Allie played it cool and nice and Brett bought it.

And all Allie'd had to lie about was having been inside and already been denied a copy of the police report. She was sure that'd happen anyway and that she'd need Rowan or someone to get it for her. So it was an inconsequential lie.

Nothing compared with all that Brett was, and had been, lying to her about.

But apparently her act wasn't as good as she'd thought, because Brett knew something was up—still, it was good enough for Brett to let it go.

Allie didn't let Brett go, though. She followed her, and this time figured her out enough in advance so as to leave her with a nice, big lead, enough of a lead so she never suspected Allie was following her.

And when Brett was at the theater, Allie decided she didn't trust Brett anymore and she realized that not only did she have to get some food some time today, but also that if she were going to continue following Brett, there was a great big likelihood that

Brett would see her, notice her.

So when she went out to get a burger, she also went to a spy store to pick up some bugs, and when she returned to the theater after finishing her burger and fries, the guard never noticed when she slipped over the fence to plant a bug in the wheel well of Brett's SUV.

The guard didn't see her going, either. Or coming back to bug Victoria's car, after Victoria got back from her lunch. Or even when she went across the street, dressed in a shitty old coat and hiding behind a newspaper with a pair of binoculars, so she could look into Brett's office. She didn't do so very successfully, but at least she wasn't caught at it.

And her distance from her car was the only reason she wasn't glued on Brett's tail when Brett left the theater. In fact, she was so caught off guard, she wasn't at her car yet when Victoria got to hers and took off after Brett, so Allie got to Luke and Laura's late enough to pull up after Victoria arrived and set up her own surveillance of the house.

So Allie watched Brett. And she watched Luke and Laura's house. And she watched Victoria watching all of that, too.

She even got to watch whoever else was watching Luke and Laura's house—it looked like two large white males—creep up to the house and keep an eye on Victoria, who'd also crept up to the house.

The guys seemed to enjoy something going on in the house and Allie wished she could see what was happening inside.

But then everyone rushed away from the house, so Allie ducked down in her car before watching first Victoria take off, then Brett.

For all Allie could tell, Victoria wasn't so much watching Brett as watching out for Brett. She wasn't following her, since she was arriving at places before Brett. So she knew beforehand where Brett was going, so was somehow on the *inside* of things.

Now that made Allie angry—very, *very* angry indeed. By the

time she was following Brett again—this time again not knowing where Brett was headed until she was nearly there—she was imagining herself as Bruce "You wouldn't want to see me when I'm angry" Banner.

Brett went home and started playing that damned Wii game again, gleefully punching out, shooting and blowing up gangsters with an intensity Allie found familiar. She watched as Brett pulled some bits and pieces of food out of a napkin, as if she didn't want to stop playing long enough to actually eat, and thought about going out to get some food for Brett.

Then Victoria showed up with a bag of what looked like food.

That was enough.

Allie drove up to the corner, turned, parked, turned off the car, and made her way back to Brett and her home, carefully sneaking while trying to look not so sneaky, until she was on her knees on the front porch, peering in through the window to watch Brett and Victoria eating salads and bread and talking.

Allie didn't like it one bit—she could never get Brett to eat any goddamned salads.

She only wished she could read lips, because it looked as if Victoria said something Brett liked and Allie wished she knew what it was. Victoria cleaned up Allie's kitchen as Brett went to her office and looked up something online.

Allie sneaked up to the office, peering through the window. She heard some barking from close by and realized the neighbor's dog was staring at her.

"Astro! Shhh!" she ordered, and he began wagging his tail so hard it was like his tail was wagging him.

She watched as Brett and Victoria looked at stuff on the Web, jotting notes and printing something out. Then Brett pulled out the computer and backpack she'd brought home from her brother's house.

Because she knew how Brett thought, Allie knew Brett would immediately hook up the CPU and start going through it. She wasn't sure what it was supposed to prove or not prove, but she knew that would be the starting point. She couldn't think of anything that would make Brett go for something else first.

But when Brett went right for the books in the bag as the starting point of her investigation, Allie remembered Brett always needed someone else to do the computer digging for her, since she wasn't that great with computers herself and could definitely not get through anyone's firewalls, passwords, or much else.

But then Brett put the books on her worktable while she went downstairs. Allie began to work her way around to keep an eye on Brett, until she realized Victoria was hooking up the computer to the monitor in Brett's office. She couldn't believe Brett was letting Victoria play with her computer!

So she kept an eye on Victoria until Brett rejoined her, bringing up a box from the basement and pulling out a case from the closet.

And then Allie couldn't believe what she was seeing—it looked like Brett was dusting the books for fingerprints—as well as several things from the box from the basement and the new computer. It also looked like she took her own prints and Victoria's and was comparing them to any from the computer and books.

And she was shaking her head.

Allie wondered if she could even go home that night, or if she'd just keep on a 24/7 stakeout of Brett.

Chapter Seventeen

"No, Brett," Victoria said. "I don't think any of these match the ones from the locket but yours."

"Well, you're not a fingerprint professional or specialist or whatever, now, are you?"

"No, but I did do those little 'Which of these is not like the other?' games when I was younger, and none of these look anything like any of those."

"Okay, fine. So maybe she didn't touch these books or this computer."

"Which is likely if she didn't, say, own them or ever touch them."

"Well, maybe I'm not remembering everything right," Brett said. "Or maybe someone cleaned them off, wiped them down or something else. Either the books and computer or this locket and these books."

"That is so more likely than, say, your cousin never having been in Luke and Laura's house."

"Glad you're seeing things my way."

"You do make a lot more sense. But still . . ." Victoria trailed off, as if she didn't want to be Brett's voice of reason.

Brett stared at her. "Why don't I see if Frankie can check with the coppers and see if they've got Merry's prints on file?"

"Yes. That might make sense. And from what you've said, they might actually have them."

"Since chances are good that she got arrested at least once for possession, prostitution, stealing or something else."

Victoria nodded. "That's what I was thinking. To make things easier, we can give 'em any prints off the computer or books that aren't yours or mine, or the set off your stuff we think are hers."

"But you're thinking she's not alive."

Victoria sat on the arm of Brett's chair, barely able to put any weight at all on it, just enough to sit next to Brett and slip an arm around her. "I'm sorry, Brett, but no. I don't think she is."

"I'll give you a call tomorrow if I need anything, otherwise I'll see you at work."

"I'm sorry, Brett, I—"

"I need to be alone now."

Victoria'd apparently figured out that she needed to listen to Brett and take what she said seriously, because she got up, grabbed her coat and went to the door. "Call me if you need any-thing," she said before leaving.

As soon as Victoria left, Brett Googled Marie and didn't find anything. She double-checked the fingerprinting and couldn't find the match she was hoping for, praying for.

But she picked up the phone and called Frankie. "Yo, Kurt, Frankie there?"

"Brett. Whatcha need?" Frankie asked, picking up the phone. Brett could hear the TV in the background.

"I need you to check with your police buddies and see if you can get prints for my brother Luke, his wife Laura or my cousin, Marie Higgins."

"Kurt—ya got paper and a pen?" Frankie said, barely covering the receiver before saying into it, "Um, is there any reason ya need these prints?"

"Yeah. I want to compare them to some that I've got."

"Should I ask where you got these prints from?"

"Some stuff I had and some stuff I got from Luke and Laura's house."

"Luke and Laura?" Kurt said, right into the phone, making it obvious he'd picked up an extension. "Weren't they like, the *it* couple from *General Hospital*?"

"They're my brother and sister-in-law," Brett said.

"You're kidding, right?" Kurt said.

"No, she's not. Now can we finish talking?" Frankie said.

"I'm just listening. Now, you wanted Luke's, Laura's and your cousin Marie's prints, right?" Kurt said, making it obvious he was taking notes. "And you want them to compare to some you've got. Should I even ask how you took the prints?"

"I bought a kit to take 'em with a while back," Brett said, pouring herself a Scotch.

"Why'd you do that?" Frankie asked.

"It made sense," Brett said. "If we were going to keep making like we were being PIs, I figured I might as well get some real PI-type equipment."

"That makes a strange sort of sense," Kurt said, then, eagerly, "What else did you get?"

"Nothing yet, but I'm going shopping tomorrow."

"Oooo, can I come with?"

"No," Frankie said. "Tell ya what, Brett. I'll get those prints for you tomorrow, if my people can get them, and if you e-mail me what you've got, I can also get 'em to compare those with their databases."

"Well, the trouble is that some of those would be mine and

Victoria's."

"Yo, dude, no problem. If I trust somebody enough to ask them for help, then I can trust them not to try something stupid 'cause I give 'em your prints. It'd be good if you let me know which yours are so my guys can eliminate them."

"True that. I'll scan 'em in and send them to you."

"Brett," Kurt said. "Tell me: Are you alone?"

"Yes, I am," she said. She wanted to add that she was alone except for the nightmares and ghosts, but she didn't. Instead she said her good-byes, then hung up and sat back with her Scotch, sipping it while she scanned in the fingerprints and e-mailed them to Frankie.

She wanted to believe Merry was alive, but she didn't, not really. It was much more likely that Luke and Laura were pretending Merry'd been kidnapped so as to try to get money out of Brett. They'd get her to pay the ransom, then make off with her money. Or pretend someone else had. Laura had explained it all nicely, but it still didn't add up. She couldn't believe it. Well, she could and did, but it didn't make sense.

Luke was trading on her hopes that Merry somehow had lived. And that made her want to see him dead more now than ever before.

Unless, of course, he did in fact cough up Merry. But how could she play this so as to find out for sure?

She opened up her notebook about the murders and looked at it. Nothing about the MOs or signatures made her think this perp would possibly go to kidnapping, or that any of it ever had anything to do with money, and kidnapping was usually about money. Or wanting to kill someone and disguise it as something else.

Yes, Laura had given several reasons and explanations, but Brett was looking for verification of some sort. None of the killings or this kidnapping made much sense. This was the stupidest case she'd ever worked, which made a weird sort of sense, since it involved the stupidest victims ever and the stupidest reason ever for her getting involved.

Regardless, why'd Luke and Laura bring her in in the first place, then? If they'd brought her in to defraud her of the ransom money, they'd taken an awfully big risk and killed a lot of people for a *chance* to get some money out of her.

But she had no way to know for sure that she was right, that Luke and Laura were in this only for her money, and she couldn't risk Merry's life on it all—her being right and them playing her.

Until she remembered that Laura'd referred to Marie as Merry, *before* Brett had. There was no way Laura could've known that. Well, there was a slight off chance that Luke would've known and remembered that, but that was an extremely off chance.

It was far more likely that Laura'd heard her use that name with her mother, actually. And maybe even grilled her about it. Or asked Luke about it.

So that meant that Brett'd been brought in, *then* this kidnapping plot developed. Or else she'd been brought in with this kidnapping plot in mind—like, if Luke was out to get her cash and had told Laura whatever he knew about her relationship with Merry and that the multiple deaths were a reason to pull her in. Like they plotted it all after the fact.

Brett pulled out the letters that had been in the box she'd brought from the basement—the letters Merry had written to her when she was in college. Back then, Brett hadn't known druggies or street people or anything like that. If she had, maybe she would've known about Merry sooner. 'Course, had she known, she might've given everything up to help Merry. But she didn't and she hadn't and maybe that was part of why she'd made it out alive and made it this far.

Brett,
It's been too long since I've seen you. I had to call Michigan State's

directory assistance to find you, but then I couldn't afford to call you. I'd like to come visit, but I don't know if I could afford that either.

I remember those few nights we spent together and wish there could be more like them, but I can't afford to come visit you or go to school up there, either. I'd ask if you could spare some money so I could come visit you, but I don't have any place for you to send the money to.

I miss you and wish we could be together again.

Love,

Merry

Brett read the letter and wished she could turn back the years and bring Merry to her. She knew now that Merry wanted to ask her for the money to come and live with her, wanted Brett to support her, but couldn't because she had nowhere for Brett to send the money to, and also knew that Brett had always dreamed of escaping to college and beyond.

She probably knew that trying to crash on Brett's dream would end it all for both of them, so she gave up so Brett could keep fighting.

Brett downed her Scotch then went upstairs, hoping to sleep, but worrying she'd have to drink a lot more before she could.

When the phone rang, she was glad she hadn't drunk any more than she had.

"Yes?" she said into the phone while sitting up.

"Thought you might like to know," Frankie said, "when I called one of my Detroit guys, they said they'd look 'em up, so I sent them your e-mail and all that shit, and Ben called back right away, saying your brother Mark'd just gotten himself killed down in Greektown. They were lucky the VIN was still readable on the engine."

"What happened?" Brett asked.

"He fell asleep with the engine on. Car blew up. Don't look like he tried to get out at all. They used the VIN and your brother Peter identified him. 'Course, they need to check it all out still."

"So he might've been dead when it blew up?"

"Might've."

"I can tell you, he didn't kill himself," Brett said.

"There were witnesses, several high school students. It sounds like he was dead when it went kaboom."

"So that happened when?"

"Just a few hours ago."

"What time?"

"Eleven thirty-seven p.m."

"Greektown."

"Yes."

"My guy's never hit two in a row like this."

"I know," Frankie said. "That's why I wanted you to know about this right away."

"Laura let me know about the last one."

"I know that, too."

"How'd they know Mark was my brother?"

Brett could practically hear Frankie shrug. "I asked him and he pulled you up. I guess somewhere in the police records you're all hooked together. I assumed it was from some complaints from when you were younger."

"I think whoever did it did this to, like, mark his territory," Kurt said, breaking the awkward silence.

"I didn't know he was on the other line," Frankie said.

"Oh, like you thought I'd let this go by without commentary!" Kurt said.

"I thought you might," Frankie said.

"So you're implying that *whoever* did this was pissed 'cause somebody else killed somebody and tried to make it look like his work?" Brett asked.

"Yup," Kurt said.

"Well, that's real messed up."

"Hey, it's your family," Kurt said.

"Yeah, it is," Brett said. "It's why I didn't talk to any of 'em for decades."

"I'd say it's more that you replaced them," Kurt said. "What do you think Frankie and me and Allie are?"

"And not Victoria?"

Kurt actually *hissed*. "No! She's the spawn of the devil!"

Brett hung up and went downstairs to play the Godfather. After she took over another family's warehouse, she went back into her study and added Mark and his death to her notebook and charts, again looking for whatever it was she was missing.

Chapter Eighteen

November 13

The next morning Brett got up, showered, thought about Merry, showered again, and got dressed in much more normal clothes—jeans and a T-shirt with a sweater. Comfortable clothes. Clothes she could breathe in. She pulled on her combat boots and leather trench, figuring she'd hit a drive-thru for breakfast before she went to the spy store.

She knew she'd be much better able to explain what she needed at the store, and pay a fair price for it, if she entered negotiations on a full stomach. Or at least with a fed body.

"Can I help you, sir?" someone asked Brett shortly after she walked into the store.

"Yes," Brett said, turning around and looking down at him. "I'm running a surveillance op. I need cameras and microphones and all that shit—y'know, bugs that I can plant in my br . . . in my suspect's home. So I can watch and tape what happens there."

"Well, first off, you do realize that taping or bugging someone without their knowledge and without a warrant is against the law, correct?"

"Yes, of course. I'm not actually doing this, y'know. I'm simply posing it as a potential situation and wondering what might help me meet my objectives."

"You seem to know what you want and what you need," the salesperson said. "Over here we have our surveillance gear. You can ask me for the prices, since, as you can see, we don't list them. We want to make sure that people know the laws before they ask or even try to buy."

"I need audio/visual equipment, complete with recording capabilities, for the six rooms of my home," Brett said. She'd already looked into everything a bit the night before, when she couldn't sleep. So now she knew about what she needed.

The sales clerk took her through the options and she made her decisions.

"Of course, if you're going to this length to be sure of what's happening in your own home, I need to wonder if you've thought about your vehicular security," the clerk asked. "For instance, we offer a wide array of vehicle tracking devices."

After he'd made that sale with Brett—in fact, she bought enough to track several vehicles, since she wanted to make sure she was set for any cars and/or suitcases/briefcases that might come into play—he looked at Brett, apparently figuring her for an easy mark, and said, "I'm wondering if you've considered your own home *security*."

"I've got a security system that I actually arm, unlike most others."

"Ah, the voice of experience," said a dapper-looking man who came from the back room. "You sound like you know what you're talking about."

Brett could smell the BS from a mile away. She stared at the new player. "What're you suggesting?"

The new player, who Brett assumed was the boss, went on to recommend several anti-bug devices and other "counterintelligence measures."

Brett picked out a few items, then looked at the new guy. "Tell you what, set me up for a credit account."

As soon as he started hemming, hawing and pulling out the paperwork, as if he was making her a deal, she put it on.

"I want a fifteen percent discount right now off all this. I want that as a condition of buying *all* this. Next up, I want a twenty percent discount if, in the next month, I give you a thousand dollars or more of additional business."

"I'm sorry, but I—"

"Last night, when I decided to make this purchase, I looked up all the shops in this area that sell this sort of equipment," Brett said. "I was gonna pay retail until you stepped in. Your clerk there, I woulda paid him. Now I'm ready to go elsewhere unless you give me a professional discount." She leaned over the counter, making sure the guy saw her .357.

"Guns ain't nothing new to me, so you aren't going to intimidate me with that one," the manager said.

"Didn't think they were. Thought you'd be more scared by me walking out of here without buying all this shit," Brett said, turning and walking toward the door.

"Wait! Okay, so here's the deal—use a credit card or something you've already got, and get *everything* you picked out, and I'll give you our fifteen percent professional discount. I'll also give you a coupon for a discount off our professional services. We can do the math and work out how much that should be, what with all you're buying today."

"You know you're gonna be real happy with this," Brett said, walking back to the counter. She thought she actually might use their professional services, and she hadn't even considered it until she came in today.

As she checked out she told the manager she needed full

background checks on two people. She knew she'd be able to tell from that how good they were.

But still she let the management dude talk her into buying a few more things. After all, she was willing to bet Allie'd come back to her and want to be a PI, and if that did happen, this would all be useful.

She hated wasting money, even though she had a lot of it, and knowing these purchases made a lot of sense helped justify it all in her mind.

And made her think about the risks folks took to justify expenditures and risks—especially when they thought they could win a helluva lot more.

Brett spent a bit at the office playing with her new toys, practicing setting them up and seeing how they all worked. Victoria helped.

Brett kinda wished she could've called in a real computer geek, like Leisa, but knew she didn't have time, so she went with what she had.

But she did take Victoria with her to Luke and Laura's house, saying she could use the extra person to help her plant bugs, which was actually the truth. Before they left the office, she drew Victoria a diagram of Luke and Laura's house, and they discussed where all they should plant which bugs and why.

When Brett went knocking, Laura answered the door.

"Well, hello, stranger!" Laura said, far too cheerfully. "Happy birthday!" She hugged Brett and kept on hugging her, regardless of Brett trying to tell her, physically, that this was not okay.

"Yeah, whatever," Brett said, finally pushing Laura away.

"Look what I made you!" Laura said, running into the kitchen and returning with a cake. "We were going to invite you over later for a surprise party, but I guess that's spoiled now." She looked over at Victoria and said, "As soon as I saw you two, I didn't think I could get Brett back here today."

"I didn't get a copy of the note yesterday," Brett said.

"Copy of the note? What note?" Laura said, dishing up the cake.

"The ransom note," Brett said. "That is, if you're still saying that my cousin Marie got kidnapped."

"Of course we are! She did!"

"And when's the drop?" Victoria asked, walking around the main area.

"Tomorrow morning," Laura said, pouring them all coffee. "I told Brett that yesterday."

"Yeah, you did. Now that copy?" Brett said.

"Let me get it from the office," Laura said. "Make yourself . . . your*selves* . . . at home." She turned to Victoria. "I'm sorry, I didn't—"

"Her name's Victoria. And we're not here for small talk or cake. I need that note," Brett said. She glanced over the room, then at Victoria, giving her a small nod before slipping a bug on the underside of the back of a shelf.

Victoria shook her head, so Brett pulled it back just as quick.

Victoria planted one under the couch, but, since no one was watching, was able to spend a few seconds placing it so as to tilt it upward.

"Well, who do we have here?" Luke said, rolling into the room on his wheelchair. "Brett! My God, little sister, you are a sight for sore eyes!" He had a big smile on his face.

If everything inside Brett wasn't screaming to *run* and *get away*, she might have bought his act for a second or two. But she knew him, so she didn't.

"Are *you* Brett's brother?" Victoria said, standing so she looked down at Luke. "Not what I imagined. Excuse me while I go to the john." With that she slipped out of the room.

At that moment, Brett kinda loved Victoria, because Victoria'd given Luke a solid putting-down, but yet, she'd left

Brett alone with him.

Brett didn't care so much for that. But still she, too, stood and looked down at her brother. "Well, ain't you a right holy roller now?"

"I've learned my lesson, little sister. I wasn't the nicest brother before, or the nicest person. I needed to learn and grow and I've done that. And I helped our cousin Marie do that, too. I was hoping the rest of our family could earn their salvation as well, and I was hoping I could be a vessel of that. But apparently that isn't meant to be."

"What do you mean?"

"Well, sister, they're all dying. Being killed. Before they can be cleansed in the eyes of our Lord."

"Yeah," Brett said, walking around the room and touching this and that, all while keeping an eye on Luke. "Like I believe any of you can ever be good or right or *cleansed in the eyes of our Lord.*"

"Please, sister, do not make fun of the faith."

"I'm not. I'm making fun of you, 'cause I don't trust a damned thing you or your wife are saying." She wanted to run. She wanted to throw up. She wanted to run and throw up. Seeing him was scaring her to her very core and making her shake in her boots like facing no number of armed men ever did.

Seeing any of her family ever again was her worst nightmare, and she was repeatedly reliving it all these days.

She needed to puke.

Luke stared at her from across the room and Brett was suddenly entirely sure that everything he was pretending to be was a lie. She had been all along, but now she was absolutely positive.

She wondered what she could do to get him up and running. What could she do to show him for the lying cheat he was?

She suddenly thought of all the classic movies she'd seen which turned the cons back on the con men, and wondered if she could plot out such an intrigue.

"This is it," Laura said, handing Brett a black-and-white photocopy of a note.

"What color was it written in?" Brett asked.

"Black," Laura said. "Like it looks. We've got a color copier."

"At home," Brett said. "Isn't that interesting." She glanced over the note. "Cocky son-of-a-bitch, handwrote this."

"Probably knew we cherish Marie too much to bring the police in," Luke said. "We wouldn't risk her life."

"And it's only the cops who could do the handwriting analysis and all that crap," Brett said. She held the note out to Laura. "I want the original. You keep the copy."

"But what if—"

"If you're only gonna give it to the cops after, they can get the original from me as well as you." Brett suddenly realized that Victoria wasn't leaving her out to the lions, she was also making her stand on her own. That itself might be enough to make Brett get very angry, but she figured Victoria was also planting bugs throughout the house in the areas they had discussed.

She would, of course, be mighty pissed if it turned out Victoria had been hiding in the john for all of this and not having an underlying purpose for her vanishing act.

Brett decided to buy Victoria a little more time. She made a big show of reading the ransom note—the copy of it, while Laura brought her the original.

Dear Reverend and Mrs. Higgins:

We have your cousin and church volunteer, Marie Higgins. We picked her up outside of the food bank she volunteers at weekly.

We are prepared to kill her and dump her body where it will never be found. We will do so at the slightest provocation or deviation from the plan, say by letting the police know about this, or bringing in any outside individuals.

You may, however, bring in your sister, Brett, since we understand you've brought her in to investigate the deaths your family has recently experienced. Also, she seems to have a lot of money, and you'll need a lot of money if you ever want to see your beloved cousin again.

If you ever want to see your cousin again, go to DTW. Go to the Mickey D's in the McNamara terminal. Buy a ticket to Baltimore and use the payphones closest to the Mickey D's. Leave your briefcase containing $1 million U.S. when you leave the pay phone at 2:11 p.m. on Friday.

Have a nice day,
The Kidnappers

Brett leaned against the credenza. "Y'know, I know a lot of people who are and have been in recovery, and one of their big things is asking forgiveness of those they've wronged." With that, Brett stared at Luke.

And stared at him some more.

And even more still.

"Oh, God, Luke—you've told *me* about some of what you did to your little sister, and how sorry you are about it all, but you've never told *her* that."

Brett watched all the emotions that went over Luke's face and she knew he was still as bad and evil as ever.

She knew she could kill him right there and then. Or beat him silly. She'd think about beating him *stupid*, but she knew he was that every day of every year.

Before she had to pick something, though, Victoria reappeared and took her by the elbow. "Brett, I need to get to work, so if you've got what you came here for, we should get going."

When they were leaving, Luke made a big show of wanting hugs from both Brett and Victoria.

Victoria leaned down to hug Brett's brother and Brett saw her sneak a bug in the wheel well of his wheelchair. She remembered all the places she'd forgotten to put bugs and started getting worried.

Then she leaned down to give her brother a hug and all worries fled her head. Instead, she felt a sharp wave of nausea fly through her, making her think she was about to get sick. She held back, though, suppressing her gag reflex while she tried to figure out what overwhelmed her so.

She finally realized he smelled like he had all those many years before and it still made her want to throw up. Her nausea was an automatic gut reaction.

After Victoria and Brett left Luke and Laura's, Brett parked around the block and went back in through the unlocked back door of Luke and Laura's garage to put the tracking devices into the wheel wells of their vehicles.

Once Brett'd planted the tracking devices, she slipped back to her car. Victoria told her where she'd planted the bugs and Brett then tested them—and their audio and visual capabilities—and the tracking devices to make sure they were all working like they were supposed to.

"Fabulous," Brett said. She immediately regretted the amount of time she hung out with fags. She wasn't one to use that word, but she was quite pleased everything was working as advertised.

She was also glad she'd bought a small monitor at the spy shop to watch the input from the video bugs. Well, to be honest, she was glad she'd spent every penny she had.

Later on she'd see if she was still such a satisfied customer, of course.

Victoria didn't seem to notice anything, not even Brett's word choice. Instead she reached into her purse and produced a few small, gift-wrapped packages and a card. "I don't know what else you have planned for today or anything, so I wanted to wish you a happy birthday right now . . ." She bashfully held out the gifts and card.

"How—" Brett started.

Victoria pressed her finger against Brett's lips before she could finish, leading Brett to think about what else Victoria might have in store for her for her birthday.

When Brett and Victoria left Brett's brother's house, Victoria went into work and Brett went into one of the theater suites near their Six and Woodward HQ at the Paradise Theater.

Brett and Frankie were setting up suites in the building they'd leased for live Web cams and filming pornos. They'd already started referring to them as their Porn or Theater Suites. Pretty much, they were setting them up as cheap, fully soundproofed apartments that had some basic props and equipment, as well as refrigerators and other necessities, including cameras.

Of course, they also had round-the-clock security on these suites, since there was some expensive equipment in them. Brett had fought for them setting them up in more expensive and better areas of town, for greater security for their equipment and such, but it looked like they could pretty easily get run out of those towns for doing what they were doing.

So they were in the low-rent side of things, but still, she checked in on the work that was going on, setting up the suites to her specifications. She'd do any film editing at the theater or at home, though. Unless directors came in and could do it themselves.

Brett was planning on writing and directing their first several pornos, of course. Maybe even start up a line of lesbian pornos, even though lesbians didn't buy a lot of pornography . . . Didn't matter, though, 'cause if she made it hot and good, enough straight guys would buy it to make it worth her while.

Brett instructed the contractors on-site, slipping the manager a few bucks here and there, then leaned against the wall, as if studying the work being done, while writing herself some notes in the pocket notebook Victoria had given her with the monogrammed fountain pen Victoria had also given her.

For her birthday, Victoria had given her a variety of cool and unique pens and notebooks and notebook supplies that inspired her and made her want to write and plan and use them. A lot of the stuff was monogrammed, and Victoria had said she'd thought about holding back those items, since Brett was once more grieving that she was related to those who were her family, but then she realized Brett was who she had made herself, and thus could use these items even more now.

Brett liked the sentiment, and she loved the items—from some place she'd never heard of, called Levenger. No matter, they looked like they were high quality and handy for her, and that was what mattered.

But somehow, once again, Victoria had taken the very worst of Brett and made it into some of the best. Suddenly, for Brett, her birthday was something that brought her some happiness. She wasn't accustomed to that.

"How'd you know my birthday?" Brett had asked Victoria.

"Pammy told me," was the simple answer.

Brett now walked into the theater to check in with Frankie, have Amber type in her script and building notes, and make sure everything across all their businesses was running smoothly.

She ran up to the top floor and pretty quickly realized something was amiss. The blinds in her office were closed, so it was dark. Very dark, since she liked good blinds.

She'd barely turned on the lights when a half dozen voices called from behind her, "Happy birthday!"

Kurt ran in behind her. "I couldn't believe this was your birthday! I told Frankie, it didn't matter what you usually did or wanted—this year, we needed to remind you that there are good people—including lots of hot and naked women—who care about you, need you and want to throw a great big party in your honor!"

"You really are a nutjob, aren't you?" Brett said.

"Oh, honey, I ain't no nutjob. I'm just a fag who loves a good party! And I ain't never been at one at a nudie joint!"

"Far as I'm concerned," Frankie said, "nobody else in this whole wide world can call you lil' sis like I can."

Frankie had never called her that, nor referred to her as such, but somehow . . . it was right and it felt good. Finally things were feeling good not only in a sexy way, but in a deep-down-inside way.

She realized how prepared everyone had to be for how long and realized this meant something to them. Granted, Frankie and Kurt probably bribed any dancers there, but Kurt had taken the day off work and . . .

It all meant something to Brett, right down to the monogrammed holster she got from Frankie. It was quality leather and something she never would've bought for herself.

The perfect gift, in other words.

Later that night, Brett looked over the ransom note yet again, focusing on one bit:

Go to DTW. Go to the Mickey D's in the McNamara terminal. Buy a ticket to Baltimore and use the pay phones closest to the Mickey D's. Leave your briefcase containing $1 million U.S. when you leave the pay phone at 2:11 p.m. on Friday.

DTW was Detroit Metro Airport. To get to the Mickey D's in the McNamara terminal, she'd need to buy a ticket. She was sure that was planned so she'd go alone, but she knew she wouldn't want to do this alone, and being cheap now could cost her Merry's life or one mil, so she'd buy more than one ticket and have someone else leave something with a camera in it close enough to capture on film whoever picked up her case, even as she left a tracer and camera in her case, too.

For now, she went back out, 'cause there was something else she needed to do.

Chapter Nineteen

"Are you sure we should've invited your sister into all of this?" Laura said to Luke, who was in the en suite Jacuzzi.

"Listen, baby," Luke said, stepping out of the tub and toweling off. "You were right there with me when we figured all this out. I mean, talk about having a mil given to ya on a silver platter, y'know?"

"I know, I know, but back then I didn't have any idea how . . . how very tenacious and . . . dangerous she is."

"Aw, baby, she's a big pussy. You just gotta remember that. Keep her in her place and it'll all be good."

"Listen, Luke, when I agreed to this, you *guaranteed* me that it didn't matter what the newspapers and all of them were saying—that you *knew* your sister and how to control her. That all that mattered was that she's got a bundle. You said we could use all those murders to our advantage and take her for a ride.

That you knew how to make it happen—to use how she felt about that drugged-up hooker to our advantage."

"Hey, when have I ever steered you wrong?" Luke said. It sounded like he was trying to make the moves on Laura and she wasn't having any of it. Brett didn't want to see what was happening, though she knew she could at any point.

"Don't you dare even think about trying to take all the credit for everything we've done. It took me—me, damnit!—to get you to realize you were gonna get yourself killed if you didn't get out of the cheap crime biz your family seems to specialize in."

"Yeah, but baby, it was all my sweet-talking that made you pick me." Now it sounded as if he'd pulled her down to the bed.

Brett glanced at her portable TV and realized she had enough video footage to prove he was no more disabled than she was, but she wanted the full and complete story before she took off and went home. Now that she was sure the entire kidnapping plot was a scam, she wanted to fry their asses for even getting her hopes up, let alone for trying to take *her* for a ride. She'd show them who the boss was, once and for all.

"But goddamned if it didn't take all my talents to make you more respectable and better talking. So you—and I—could make full use of your talents so we both could benefit."

"Well hot damn, woman. If our people ever heard you talking like that, we wouldn't take in nearly the money we do. Remember, we are the holy types."

"Holy rollers. Fuck, Luke, if they ever saw you walking—"

"We'd make 'em think it was a goddamned miracle. Plain and simple."

"But I should've gone with my instincts, like always. They've never steered us wrong."

"They were hardly right before we hooked up, babe. You were working in the jailhouse infirmary, for Christ's sake."

"Yes, but at least I was on the right side of the gates when night came."

"Except when you were working the night shift."

Laura gave a little scream that made Brett very happy indeed that she had switched off her TV. She could only imagine what was going on in their bedroom, just like she could only imagine what they did at night in the prison's infirmary.

Actually, she didn't even want to imagine that. After all, she was on a stakeout and she hadn't brought a bucket with her.

But she was recording everything. She wasn't sure if any of it would be admissible in court, but she was sure that if it wasn't, she'd find some other, equally purposeful use for it. She didn't like frauds, con men or swindlers, and she especially didn't like it when the evildoers were posing as religious types. She didn't like religion regardless, since she always saw it as a form of scam from the get-go, but when supposedly religious types used their position to defraud believing types she was particularly disgusted. Especially when those getting the shirts taken from their backs were little old folks who had been taught to believe and trust in anyone who wore a collar or anything remotely like one.

It figured that her brother had worked out a legal way to take such advantage of some of the most susceptible people in society—and make it seem as if they were helping the most worst-off in the world.

She wanted to bring them down—Luke, Laura and the whole stupid, arrogant, egotistical and . . . and . . . well, downright evil herd of 'em.

But first she wanted the rest of the story. She figured she could eventually torture it out of 'em, and that'd be a lot of fun, but she reckoned life in prison would be a lot more fun for them. Not as much for her, but she wanted torture, pain and humiliation for her brother and his wife.

She thought about Helen Anderson and the trust in her wide-eyed gaze and realized she wanted a *lot* of torture, pain and humiliation, with death, for her brother and his wife.

Luke and Laura were apparently done with whatever they'd

been doing. It sounded as if Luke was going to sleep, but Laura wasn't quite ready for it. Brett listened for a moment before turning the TV back on and flipping through her cameras before she found the one she wanted.

Now she could see Laura come back in with two bottles of beer. She was wearing a short, black robe. Not exactly what Brett would have expected from a holy person. Luke and Laura apparently spared no expense as far as their personal comfort was concerned.

Laura lay next to Luke on the bed and handed him a beer. "I don't like that your sister took things from our house. If she's as tight with the law as she supposedly is, she might figure out that I've never met your cousin."

"She's a dyke who wants her incestual little playbuddy back. She ain't gonna pay no attention but what her pussy wants."

"You really are a disgusting pig."

"And you love me for it."

"Despite it."

"You were the one who let little what's-her-face walk out of here with half our props."

"What the fuck was I supposed to do? She scares the fuck outta me! And I bet she would bring the cops down on our asses if she found out anything about us!"

Brett smiled about that. She was happy to know that she did what she intended to do. She liked knowing she could scare the crap outta the bad guys. Granted, it was better when they were big guys who were scary themselves, but it was nice knowing that she scared a woman who realized her brother Luke was wholly and totally controllable.

"But she's not going to figure out anything about us," Luke said.

"She'd better not. I believed you when you suggested this—"

"Hey, something like this only happens once in a lifetime, so we might as well use it."

"Somebody's out there killing half your family—"

"Might all be accidents."

"Not so many in such quick succession. Luke, I'm really afraid for my life!"

"Yeah, right. You're even safer with little what's-her-face on the case. She's gonna figure out who's doing it quicker than any cops would."

"You're not concerned at all, are you?" Laura asked.

"No. Babe, we've got boatloads of security. We're the safest Higginses of all, what with our twenty-four/seven security detail. We ain't got nothing to worry about."

"So you say. I'm not so sure. I mean, you've never been so sure that it's a serial killer, but I know better. I've worked in prisons."

"And I've been in prisons. Listen, we've got Brett right where we want her—" Luke said.

"No, no we don't. Where we want her is handing us her money, and she's not doing that."

"*Yet*. She's not doing it *yet*!"

"You made this all sound like cake, and it so ain't seeming cake to me! Luke, we murdered someone—"

"We didn't have a choice. We need to do that escalation thing you were talking about, and we needed to add in some immediacy and all that shit."

Brett realized Laura was the brains behind the op. No wonder some things weren't feeling totally right to her—it was because Laura was teaching Luke. Maybe all the main ideas were Luke's, but Laura was filling in the blanks for him. She must've picked up some criminal psychology while she worked in the big house.

And then Brett realized that Luke and Laura had killed at least one person to help keep her in the game. She knew she should be upset by that, but it was one more Higgins off the planet, and that was a good thing.

But from what all she was hearing, there *was* a serial killer on the loose, and Luke and Laura had *only* killed one of the people and faked Merry's kidnapping. On top of all their general frauds and all, that was. So she was only partway to resolution. She wondered who really was killing off all her relatives.

"It'll all work out, baby," Luke said to Laura.

Laura slapped Luke. "You bastard! You promised me that we'd get even richer from this! You promised it'd make everything we've done look like nothing! Well, I ain't seeing that! What I *am* seeing is that she's somebody who can bring this entire goddamned house of cards down on us!"

"Yo, yo, yo, baby. I know what you set up for us, 'kay, baby? And I ain't in no way about to risk all of that."

Brett smiled at the monitor and thought about how he had already put everything they had at risk.

And that was when the glass cruncher smashed through the window at her side and a massive arm reached through and grabbed her, smashing her head against the door frame.

Chapter Twenty

Brett could practically feel her eyes rolling up in her head when she reached into her holster, grabbed her gun, pointed it in the general direction of her assailant, heard a gunshot, thought she was dead, and pulled the trigger.

It took her a moment after she felt the warm liquid dripping down her cheek to realize that it was her assailant's blood and not hers. This fact, and the awareness that she'd have his hand marks around her neck, made her know she could claim this as self-defense.

Also, a lot of people knew Laura'd asked her to investigate the deaths in the family, something which should justify anything she'd done, down to investigating and bugging Luke and Laura's.

No matter what the actual laws were, she knew she could prove her actions and justify her reactions.

They'd sent someone out to kill her, after all.

Brett hit the gas and pulled out, figuring it'd make things a lot better for her after the fact than if she claimed this body right here and now.

She now knew that Luke and Laura had pulled her in, hoping to get money out of her. Also, they'd killed at least one person and had defrauded hundreds or thousands out of thousands or millions. In order to really know how much damage they'd done, she'd have to see if they had a radio, TV, Web or mail ministry tied into the Ministry of the Healing Hand. New technology made it so much easier and more efficient getting stupid people to open their wallets so you could defraud them.

And her main wonderment as far as this was concerned was what would give the cops enough to go in and investigate them. Could she just drop a tip to the IRS, or would it take a copy of her A/V footage, or copies of what she'd copied when she was there . . .

And that was it. She'd claim Helen Anderson had given her copies of various financial files for her work, and she'd looked into them.

She only needed to give to the cops enough to make them seriously look into the church. Enough to make them analyze the financial dealings.

And she had that.

Of course, they were only claiming the murder of *one* of her relatives, so she still had to worry about who killed the rest of them, particularly Mark, whose murder seemed to be a real vengeance killing. Someone wasn't happy anyone else was claiming credit for the rest of the murders.

But if the guy she'd killed moments ago had coworkers, or some sort of direct link to Luke and Laura—like maybe being one of the security detail they'd referred to—the jig might already be up. She swung a U-ie and went back to the scene of the crime, where she hopped out of her SUV to look down at the guy and realize there was no way she was touching his ugly corpse.

She immediately called Victoria, wanting to make sure that she was all right. After all, if one of Luke and Laura's security detail attacked her because she was watching Luke and Laura's house, which only made sense that that was who he was, then if Victoria had again been watching her—

"Hello?" Victoria said, answering her phone on the second ring.

"Thank God you're all right," Brett replied, just before she called Frankie to help her move the dead guy. She didn't want to touch him, but she couldn't exactly leave him just lying there.

Chapter Twenty-one
November 14

"I've got a warrant," Randi said to Brett over the phone the next morning. "We're gonna go in and rip that joint apart, 'cause I'm right with you—I don't like people who take advantage of those who want to believe in something and want to help."

"Good," Brett said, stretching in her bed. "Did you get anything more on Mark's death?"

"It looks like he got so drunk he didn't wake up when the car caught on fire. It was a mechanical malfunction and he slept through it. The scientists and docs are still looking through it all and trying to figure it all out."

There was a beeping on Brett's phone. "Hang on a sec, 'kay, Randi?" she said before flipping over to the other line. "Yeah?"

"Brett," Peter said. "There's no way Mark killed himself."

"I think it was a goddamned accident, Pete."

"Yeah, he's such a moron, I woulda thought that, too. 'Cept I told Luke yesterday that you and me was talking about finances. And he knew you was onto him, and that I knew enough . . ."

And that was when Brett was convinced that Peter was gay, too. His secret was, of course, worse than hers—he'd been in love with Mark, and that was utterly disgusting.

God, she hated her fam. And then she started to think . . .

"I needed you to know that Mark didn't kill himself," Peter said. "I'm not even sure he died by his own stupidity."

"Peter, why are you calling me with this?"

"You know why better than anyone else in this world," Peter said, then hung up.

Brett stared at the phone for a minute, then switched back to Randi, who had already hung up.

She realized Peter was about to kill himself, and she knew she could stop it, but she didn't want to.

She now had bits and pieces of the mystery solved, but still didn't know who was killing her family. Or most of them. Peter's cryptic remark made her think that maybe he knew more than he was saying. From what he did, say, however, it seemed almost as if whoever was doing this was gay, too.

And given that it all started on Christmas Day, in the commode, and there was no mention of breaking and entering or any other crimes anywhere, it seemed as if her father was killed by someone who had every right in the world to be in her parents' house on Christmas.

It was then that she realized she didn't want to even think about what had happened.

So, instead, she stared at the ceiling a bit longer, remembering how Merry's skin felt, and how soft and warm Merry had been.

She didn't want to save her brother, and couldn't find a reason to, either.

And she knew Randi knew what she needed, and had everything Brett had. Randi knew about the fraud and the murder, and Luke not being crippled and all that.

She reached over and pulled a picture of Merry out. She lay back and remembered . . . finally allowed herself to remember why she'd been so morose so many mornings of late.

She finally remembered the last time she'd made love to Merry.

"Brett," Merry had said, coming up to Brett in the East Lansing Mickey D's, the one a block outside of Cedar Village, the off-campus housing that had bought its land early enough that it was on campus.

Brett didn't live there. She was on a scholarship and various other types of programs. At the time, she planned on going on to live in off-campus housing, but the very, very, ridiculously cheap sort that would require her to take multiple buses to and from classes, or else ride miles on her cheap bike.

Brett was happy to see the one bit of familiarity that she greeted with happiness.

"Nick," Brett said to the other manager. "Is it okay if I take a break now?"

"Yes," he said.

And Brett piled enough free food on her tray for both her and Merry. She knew Nick could narc on her for this, but she also knew she never stole food before, so they'd have to be idiots to roast her for this.

She didn't understand homophobia back then.

Brett and Merry ate, Merry diving into her food voraciously, as if she were starving. That made sense to Brett. Since Merry was so skinny, she likely was half starved.

"I didn't expect to see you up here, especially not since your letter," Brett said.

"I didn't think I could make it either, but somebody I knew was coming up here, and I wanted to see how my big college-girl cuz was doing," Merry said, putting her right hand on the table so Brett could reach out and hold it.

Brett did so. "I've missed you," she said. "A lot."

"Me you, too," Merry said.

Brett blushed and looked down at the table. She dipped another fry into some ranch dressing and threw it into her mouth. "So, um, you're staying the night up here?"

"If I can, yes."

"With me?" Brett asked hopefully.

"Either that or on a bench."

"I can't have you sleeping on a bench."

Merry looked away. "I already met your roommate. I went to your room first, of course. She was the one who told me where to find you."

"Oh, yeah. I was wondering . . . So you're okay spending the night in my dorm room?"

"I'd love to." Merry squeezed Brett's fingers with her own. "Your roomie said she'd leave us alone tonight."

Brett looked up, startled. She was sure she looked like a deer in the headlights of an oncoming car.

"Is that all right?" Merry asked, shyly.

"Yes," Brett said, gulping down her drink and making it look like she needed to get back to work, which she did need to do, but . . .

She was also thinking about being alone in her room with Merry. She didn't know what would happen there. But Merry being there was nice, in and of itself. Anything else would simply be . . . nicer.

Merry hung out at McDonald's until closing, even helping Brett and the crew clean things up before, after and during close.

Then she walked back to Hubbard Hall with Brett, first reaching out to hold Brett's hand, then leaning into Brett's shoulder and warmth. It was only then that Brett realized how pitiful Merry's jacket was, and wrapped an arm around her, feeling a bit guilty that she liked having to warm Merry like this, because she enjoyed it so much.

And all through the walk, Brett tried to figure out what to do when they got back to her dorm, not realizing that all that thought and worry were needless.

They had barely stepped inside Brett's room and closed the door behind them, with Merry taking just a moment to see the layout of the room and make sure they were alone, while Brett locked the door, before she wrapped her arms around Brett's neck.

"I've been wanting to do this all night," she said, tipping up on her toes so she could kiss Brett.

Brett practically collapsed back against the wall. Her knees got weak and her entire world almost faded to black, except it got incredibly warm.

"Merry, God, Merry," she said, holding Merry tightly against her. She couldn't believe she had Merry in her arms again . . . and . . . and . . . and . . . it was all so much and so nice and so sweet and unbelievable . . . Merry's lips were soft and sweet and her mouth was warm and wet and her tongue sent brilliant little shocks throughout Brett's entire body . . .

Merry reached up to twine her arms around Brett's neck, pushing her body up against Brett's, even while she pushed Brett's body against the wall, pressing her against it as she pressed herself against Brett.

"I should . . ." Brett said. "I should probably take a shower. I probably smell like McDonald's."

"You do. But I'll only let you take a shower if I can join you," Merry said, stepping back and dropping her light jacket to the floor. It was winter in Michigan. Brett wanted to warm Merry against herself, but then Merry unbuttoned her blouse and dropped it to the floor as well.

Her breasts were full and pert. The lights were on and Brett felt as if she should suggest they turn them down, or just turn them down herself, but she wanted to see Merry's body.

Merry leaned back against a corner, her arms pushed back so Brett could study her naked body from the waist up. Her skin was pale, her nipples pink and hard and her breasts were full and Brett wanted to touch them and hold them and kiss them and she knew it was all wrong, very, very wrong, but she wanted to, she wanted to with all her heart and soul.

She remembered how soft and sweet Merry was, to the mouth and the touch, and she wanted to experience it all yet again, but couldn't believe that Merry was going to let her yet again—

"Brett, please say something," Merry said, bringing her arms up to cover her breasts.

"My God, you're beautiful," Brett said, taking Merry's hands into her own. "So very, very beautiful." She turned to the room, looking at her bed up in its loft.

"Brett," Merry said, taking Brett's face in her hands. "You know I love you, right?"

Brett did. "Yes. I love you, too."

"I know. And I don't know what will happen tomorrow, but I know what I want to happen tonight."

Every nerve in Brett's body was twitching. She felt like an electrical circuit, a circuit box, even. "I just want to touch you."

"Don't stop touching me, ever."

"I won't. Never."

Merry took Brett's hands in her own, placing them onto the waistband of her jeans. She helped Brett undo her zipper, then slide her jeans down and off her hips and legs, until she was wearing only her panties.

She looked up at Brett. "I need to feel you. Against me and inside me."

Brett reached down to wrap Merry around her so she could carry her up to her bed.

That sounded a lot better than it was. Brett leaned back so Merry's back wouldn't scrape on the wooden ladder, but then she almost fell backward, so she pressed forward and Merry's back scraped on the ladder and she was mortified.

Merry burst out laughing. Her legs were wrapped tightly around Brett, practically gluing them together, so she was able to play with Brett's hair with her hands. "You're butch, not a miracle worker. Take me to bed, woman, and make love to me."

"Are you laughing at me?"

"Yes, yes I am."

Brett carried her the rest of the way and ripped her panties off, lying on top of her, pressing into her, kissing her and feeling her. Merry unbuttoned, pushed, pulled and otherwise ripped Brett's clothing off,

217

even as they kissed and Brett licked her way down Merry's body, enjoying the warmth, the closeness, and the way Merry writhed under her, pushing up against her and wiggling to get her into the perfect position.

Brett moved down her body, taking her time worshipping every inch of her wonderful body, licking and nibbling on her skin, her nipples, her tummy and down . . .

And she could feel Merry's increasing wetness against her tummy, her chest . . . and then her hand and fingers.

She coated her hand and fingers in Merry, and then slid a finger up and into her.

"Oh, God, yes," Merry said, squirming against her.

And then Brett slid her tongue against Merry, tasting her clit from bottom to top and back down again, all the while working her finger in and out.

Then she slid a second finger in as well, and began working her tongue back and forth across Merry's clit.

Merry opened her legs wider still, letting Brett in all the way, letting Brett take her however she wanted.

Brett thrust two fingers in and out and in and out and in and out again, while she worked her tongue back and forth, over and over, and then snaked her other hand up over Merry's naked skin—her naked belly, her bare breasts, her exposed and tender nipples. She fondled and tweaked one nipple, then the other, cupping each breast in turn, and enjoying the view as Merry stretched out to grasp the bookshelf over her head, giving Brett a total and unobstructed view of her beautiful, naked body.

Brett could tell as it all became more and more urgent to Merry. And she took Merry there, enjoying each and every moment of it, relishing the sight and feel of Merry, not quite believing she was with Merry like this, just how she'd always dreamed, yet again.

"Brett, oh God, Brett, yes, yes . . ."

Brett slipped another finger into Merry, even as she licked her harder and faster. She wanted them to be together like this always, and she never wanted to let Merry go.

When Brett woke up, she realized she'd gotten fully into the dream. So much so her fingers were in her boxers and they and her boxers were a bit wet and sticky.

She'd blocked it out for years. That last time she'd been with Merry. Back then, she was ashamed of everything sexual in her life, but apparently she was especially ashamed about being with Merry, since she'd blocked it out of her mind.

Either that or she still couldn't believe that had been the last time they'd been together. She'd made love to Merry several times that night, as if she didn't want the night to end, because the next day would come, and it might all end.

And it did.

When Brett had woken the next day, Merry was gone.

Brett was glad her last thought was of them falling asleep together, with Merry in her arms.

And now, knowing what she did, Brett had to stop. If Merry was already on the junk, it would've made sense for her to have hitchhiked up to East Lansing to see Brett, and then stolen whatever she could from Brett, but she hadn't taken a single nickel from Brett.

Which meant that Merry had gone up to say good-bye to Brett.

Brett rolled over and cried.

Chapter Twenty-two

The next morning, Brett stopped by her mother's house again. She just needed resolution to this whole torrid affair, and then she'd sail off into a happily-ever-after where she never saw any of her family ever again. Before she went in, though, she walked around the house, scoping the sitch. Behind the house, she found one of her nephews, one of the ones she'd recently beaten up. As soon as he saw her, he slipped the book he'd been reading into his jacket pocket. That is, the inside pocket of his oversized and overworn denim jacket, a jacket that didn't stand any chance against the brutal Michigan winters.

She slipped out next to him, sidling next to him on the frozen ground. "Whatcha reading?" she asked.

"Reading? What the fuck'd I be doing reading?"

"Saw you with the book. Now hand it over."

"Goddamned bitch."

Brett stared at him for a moment and realized how much appearances meant to him. She pulled out her gun and put it to his head. "Hand over the goddamned book."

"You oughta know better'n anybody that I won't." He looked up at her. "I'm willing to kill to hide my secrets."

Brett stared down at him and realized that he'd rather be in jail for the rest of his life than grow up with whatever he'd been growing up with.

"Who do you belong to?" she asked.

"You should know better than to ask that sorta shit in our family," he said.

"Who's your mama?"

"You met her. Chriss."

"And your daddy?"

"You know him, too. Uncle Frank. I'm your cousin Marie's brother."

Brett sat, looking down at him. "Is she still alive?" she asked.

"Yes."

Brett had already figured out that it was one of the kids killing everyone. She'd even decided she'd let whoever was doing it go free.

"I'm gonna let you walk away from it all now," Brett said. "But you gotta stop, 'cause next time, I won't. And don't ever lie to me again."

"You know as well as I do that they all deserve to die and need to die. If even just for killing Marie."

The one thing she wasn't sure of was if he was telling the truth about his mother and father. She knew he was lying when he said that Marie wasn't dead.

"Yeah, I do. And that's why you're walking away now. But the cops'll find you if you keep at it, so you gotta stop."

"You're the only one who's got any reason to look twice at us—"

"*Us?* You mean your bro's in on it, too?"

"You are as stupid as everyone else in this family, ain't you?"

Brett was having a real bad day, so her hand was already on her gun, pulling it out, when she felt the barrel of a gun against her temple.

She froze.

"You probably never even figured out that you don't have the same dad as your brothers," Bobby said.

She reached up, grabbed Bobby's weapon and turned it back on him before she realized it was a goddamned water pistol.

"We have nothing against you, *Auntie* Brett," Jack said, standing and looking at her.

"If we actually were, or thought we were, the badasses everyone else thinks we are," Bobby said, "then we would."

"We haven't come for you because you don't deserve it," Jack said.

"So, like, are you two psychopaths?" Brett said, not putting her gun away.

"No," Jack said.

"We're not," Bobby said.

"Your father tried to attack me last Christmas in the john," Jack said.

Bobby shrugged. "I heard them, came in, and hit your father with the door when I came in. He fell and cracked his skull on the john."

"That's when we figured out what we could do, and what we had to do, if we were gonna survive."

Brett's phone rang and she answered it.

"Omigod, omigod, Brett! Brett!" Randi said, practically crying into the phone.

That wasn't like Randi. Not at all.

"Randi, calm down and talk to me," Brett said, walking away from Jack and Bobby, the gay Higgins twins. Peter'd known they were behind it all along, but they were all gay, so all had something to hide—except for her, of course. She'd gotten away from it all.

"When we pulled in your cousins," Randi said, "they kept talking about being followed and bugged. They said one of their security detail missing the night before, and that another one caught a disturbance—found somebody watching them!"

"So what happened?" Brett asked.

"I need to know something, Brett. Did you run into any of Luke and Laura's security detail last night?"

"Some guy tried to attack me, so I knocked him out and took off. I had everything I needed by then, so there was no reason to hang out any longer."

"Aw, shit, did one of Luke's hired guns try to get it on with you?" Bobby (or was it Jackie?) asked her. The twins were apparently eavesdropping.

Brett walked away. "Why do ya ask?" she asked Randi.

"Brett, Allie didn't show up at Rowan's last night. She's missing, Brett."

"And what does this have to do with Luke and Laura?"

"We found her car outside of their place. Just down the block from them. There was a recorder on the front seat, Brett, and it was filled with her surveillance notes from this investigation. She was tailing you, Brett, and now she's missing and in one of her entries she noted that Victoria was watching you, and two guys were watching you and the house as well."

"I'm still not tracking here, Randi. Could you get to the point already? And stop saying my name, 'cause it's really creeping me out."

"Brett, Allie's missing and we found her car outside of your brother's house with its driver's window bashed in. She's missing and I'm afraid she's dead."

Publications from
BELLA BOOKS, INC.
The best in contemporary lesbian fiction

P.O. Box 10543, Tallahassee, FL 32302
Phone: 800-729-4992
www.bellabooks.com

WITHOUT WARNING: Book one in the Shaken series by KG MacGregor. *Without Warning* is the story of their courageous journey through adversity, and their promise of steadfast love.   978-1-59493-120-8 $13.95

THE CANDIDATE by Tracey Richardson. Presidential candidate Jane Kincaid had always expected the road to the White House would exact a high personal toll. She just never knew how high until forced to choose between her heart and her political destiny.
978-1-59493-133-8 $13.95

TALL IN THE SADDLE by Karin Kallmaker, Barbara Johnson, Therese Szymanski and Julia Watts. The playful quartet that penned the acclaimed *Once Upon A Dyke* and *Stake Through the Heart* are back are now turning to the Wild (and Very Hot) West to bring you another collection of erotically charged, action-packed, tales.
978-1-59493-106-2 $15.95

IN THE NAME OF THE FATHER by Gerri Hill. In this highly anticipated sequel to *Hunter's Way*, Dallas homicide detectives Tori Hunter and Samantha Kennedy investigate the murder of a Catholic priest who is found naked and strangled to death.
978-1-59493-108-6 $13.95

IT'S ALL SMOKE AND MIRRORS: *The First Chronicles of Shawn Donnelly* by Therese Szymanski. Join Therese Szymanski as she takes a walk on the sillier side of the gritty crime scene detective novel and introduces readers to her newest alternate personality—Shawn Donnelly.   978-1-59493-117-8 $13.95

THE ROAD HOME by Frankie J. Jones. As Lynn finds herself in one adventure after another, she discovers that true wealth may have very little to do with money after all.
978-1-59493-110-9 $13.95

IN DEEP WATERS: CRUISING THE SEAS by Karin Kallmaker and Radclyffe. Book passage on a deliciously sensual Mediterranean cruise with tour guides Radclyffe and Karin Kallmaker.   978-1-59493-111-6 $15.95

ALL THAT GLITTERS by Peggy J. Herring. Life is good for retired Army Colonel Marcel Robicheaux. Marcel is unprepared for the turn her life will take. She soon finds herself in the pursuit of a lifetime—searching for her missing mother and lover.
978-1-59493-107-9 $13.95

OUT OF LOVE by KG MacGregor. For Carmen Delallo and Judith O'Shea, falling in love proves to be the easy part. 978-1-59493-105-5 $13.95

BORDERLINE by Terri Breneman. Assistant Prosecuting attorney Toni Barston returns in the sequel to *Anticipation*. 978-1-59493-99-7 $13.95

PAST REMEMBERING by Lyn Denison. What would it take to melt Peri's cool exterior? Any involvement on Asha's part would be simply asking for trouble and heartache . . . wouldn't it? 978-1-59493-103-1 $13.95

ASPEN'S EMBERS by Diane Tremain Braund. Will Aspen choose the woman she loves . . . or the forest she hopes to preserve . . . 978-1-59493-102-4 $14.95

THE COTTAGE by Gerri Hill. *The Cottage* is the heartbreaking story of two women who meet by chance . . . or did they? A love so destined it couldn't be denied . . . stolen moments to be cherished forever. 978-1-59493-096-6 $13.95

FANTASY: Untrue Stories of Lesbian Passion edited by Barbara Johnson and Therese Szymanski. Lie back and let Bella's bad girls take you on an erotic journey through the greatest bedtime stories never told. 978-1-59493-101-7 $15.95

SISTERS' FLIGHT by Jeanne G'Fellers. *Sisters' Flight* is the highly anticipated sequel to *No Sister of Mine* and *Sister Lost, Sister Found*.
978-1-59493-116-1 $13.95

BRAGGIN' RIGHTS by Kenna White. Taylor Fleming is a thirty-six-year-old Texas rancher who covets her independence. She finds her cowgirl independence tested by neighboring rancher Jen Holland. 978-1-59493-095-9 $13.95

BRILLIANT by Ann Roberts. Respected sociology professor, Diane Cole finds her views on love challenged by her own heart, as she fights the attraction she feels for a woman half her age. 978-1-59493-115-4 $13.95

THE EDUCATION OF ELLIE by Jackie Calhoun. When Ellie sees her childhood friend for the first time in thirty years she is tempted to resume their long lost friendship. But with the years come a lot of baggage and the two women struggle with who they are now while fighting the painful memories of their first parting. Will they be able to move past their history to start again? 978-1-59493-092-8 $13.95

DATE NIGHT CLUB by Saxon Bennett. *Date Night Club* is a dark romantic comedy about the pitfalls of dating in your thirties . . . 978-1-59493-094-2 $13.95

PLEASE FORGIVE ME by Megan Carter. Laurel Becker is on the verge of losing the two most important things in her life—her current lover, Elaine Alexander, and the Lavender Page bookstore. Will Elaine and Laurel manage to work through their misunderstandings and rebuild their life together? 978-1-59493-091-1 $13.95

WHISKEY AND OAK LEAVES by Jaime Clevenger. Meg meets June, a single woman running a horse ranch in the California Sierra foothills. The two become quick friends and it isn't long before Meg is looking for more than just a friendship. But June has no interest in developing a deeper relationship with Meg. She is, after all, not the least bit interested in women . . . or is she? Neither of these two women is prepared for what lies ahead . . . 978-1-59493-093-5 $13.95

SUMTER POINT by KG MacGregor. As Audie surrenders her heart to Beth, she begins to distance herself from the reckless habits of her youth. Just as they're ready to meet in the middle, their future is thrown into doubt by a duty Beth can't ignore. It all comes to a head on the river at Sumter Point. 978-1-59493-089-8 $13.95

THE TARGET by Gerri Hill. Sara Michaels is the daughter of a prominent senator who has been receiving death threats against his family. In an effort to protect Sara, the FBI recruits homicide detective Jaime Hutchinson to secretly provide the protection they are so certain Sara will need. Will Sara finally figure out who is behind the death threats? And will Jaime realize the truth—and be able to save Sara before it's too late?

978-1-59493-082-9 $13.95

REALITY BYTES by Jane Frances. In this sequel to *Reunion*, follow the lives of four friends in a romantic tale that spans the globe and proves that you can cross the whole of cyberspace only to find love a few suburbs away . . .   978-1-59493-079-9 $13.95

MURDER CAME SECOND by Jessica Thomas. Broadway's bad-boy genius, Paul Carlucci, has chosen *Hamlet* for his latest production and, to the delight of some and despair of others, he has selected Provincetown's amphitheatre for his opening gala. But Alex Peres realizes the wrong people are falling down, and the moaning is all too realistic. Someone must not be shooting blanks . . .   978-1-59493-081-2 $13.95

SKIN DEEP by Kenna White. Jordan Griffin has been given a new assignment: Track down and interview one-time nationally renowned broadcast journalist Reece McAllister. Much to her surprise, Jordan comes away with far more than just a story . . .

978-1-59493-78-2 $13.95

FINDERS KEEPERS by Karin Kallmaker. *Finders Keepers*, the quest for the perfect mate in the 21st century, joins Karin Kallmaker's *Just Like That* and her other incomparable novels about lesbian love, lust and laughter.   1-59493-072-4 $13.95

OUT OF THE FIRE by Beth Moore. Author Ann Covington feels at the top of the world when told her book is being made into a movie. Then in walks Casey Duncan the actress who is playing the lead in her movie. Will Casey turn Ann's world upside down?

1-59493-088-0 $13.95

STAKE THROUGH THE HEART: NEW EXPLOITS OF TWILIGHT LESBIANS by Karin Kallmaker, Julia Watts, Barbara Johnson and Therese Szymanski. The playful quartet that penned the acclaimed *Once Upon A Dyke* are dimming the lights for journeys into worlds of breathless seduction.   1-59493-071-6 $15.95

THE HOUSE ON SANDSTONE by KG MacGregor. Carly Griffin returns home to Leland and finds that her old high school friend Justine is awakening more than just old memories.   1-59493-076-7 $13.95

WILD NIGHTS: MOSTLY TRUE STORIES OF WOMEN LOVING WOMEN edited by Therese Szymanski. 264 pp. 23 new stories from today's hottest erotic writers are sure to give you your wildest night ever!   1-59493-069-4 $15.95

COYOTE SKY by Gerri Hill. 248 pp. Sheriff Lee Foxx is trying to cope with the realization that she has fallen in love for the first time. And fallen for author Kate Winters, who is technically unavailable. Will Lee fight to keep Kate in Coyote?

1-59493-065-1 $13.95

VOICES OF THE HEART by Frankie J. Jones. 264 pp. A series of events force Erin to swear off love as she tries to break away from the woman of her dreams. Will Erin ever find the key to her future happiness?   1-59493-068-6 $13.95